W9-BFI-048

THE
PIZZA PUZZLE

Susan Beth Pfeffer

A Yearling Book

Published by
Bantam Doubleday Dell Books for Young Readers
a division of
Bantam Doubleday Dell Publishing Group, Inc.
1540 Broadway
New York, New York 10036

If you purchased this book without a cover you should be aware that this
book is stolen property. It was reported as "unsold and destroyed" to the
publisher and neither the author nor the publisher has received any pay-
ment for this "stripped book."

Copyright © 1996 by Susan Beth Pfeffer

All rights reserved. No part of this book may be reproduced or trans-
mitted in any form or by any means, electronic or mechanical, including
photocopying, recording, or by any information storage and retrieval
system, without the written permission of the Publisher, except where
permitted by law. For information address Delacorte Press, New York,
New York 10036.

The trademarks Yearling® and Dell® are registered in the U.S. Patent
and Trademark Office and in other countries.

ISBN: 0-440-41391-5

Reprinted by arrangement with Delacorte Press

Printed in the United States of America

September 1997

10 9 8 7 6 5 4 3 2 1

CWO

For Doris Mohin,
neighbor and friend

S 61 LIBRARY

S U LIBRARY

Chapter One

Sometimes you can hear whispers better than shouts.

My parents were doing the whispering. They'd been doing a lot of it lately, talking quietly so that Paul and I did not hear their voices. I was supposed to be asleep, and Paul always played the radio, so we weren't supposed to know. But we did.

I used to like it when my parents whispered. I figured they were discussing what to buy me for my birthday or for Christmas. When I was younger and we'd drive to my grandparents', I'd pretend to be asleep just so that I could hear my parents' private whispering. It made me feel as if I could see into their grown-up lives. They'd whisper

1

about vacation plans, or people they knew, or money. Sometimes, when I was very lucky, they'd whisper about Paul or me. And when I'd pretend to wake up, I'd act as if I had no idea what they'd been talking about, even though I knew their secrets.

But lately, the whispering had been angry. Paul and I weren't supposed to hear because Mom and Dad didn't want us to know that anything was wrong. As if you could keep that from your kids. As if we didn't all live in the same house.

I heard enough of the whispers to know they'd been fighting about the same stuff for weeks. Lisa's name came up a lot, and sometimes Mom almost forgot to keep her voice down. Other times their voices would get so soft that I couldn't make out the words, just an undercurrent of anger.

Mom and Dad had been having these whispering battles almost nightly now for a month. I don't know why it bothered me so much that particular night, but it did, and I tiptoed out of my room and knocked softly on Paul's door.

"Come in," he said. He was sitting at his desk doing his homework. I sat down on his bed.

"They're whispering again," I said. Paul had his radio on loud enough that he might not have known.

"I figured," he said. "Same stuff?"

"Lisa," I said. "Other things too, I think." I was pretty sure it was all Lisa, but if there were other problems, then the Lisa one might not be so serious. A half dozen minor things seemed a lot better to me than one big Lisa thing.

"What other things?" Paul asked.

"I don't know," I said. "Just stuff."

"You mean it's all Lisa," Paul said.

"I guess," I said.

Paul scowled. "Dad should either move in with her or fire her."

"Move in with her?" I asked.

"Well, if he's having an affair, he might as well," Paul said.

"Having an affair?"

"You know," Paul said. "You know what an affair is, don't you, Taryn?"

"Of course I do. I'm in seventh grade," I said, as if having affairs was one of my subjects, along with English and math. "Do you really think Dad and Lisa are . . ." I couldn't make myself say it.

"I don't know," Paul said. "Dad doesn't talk to me about stuff like that. But Mom thinks they are."

"She told you that?" I asked.

"She didn't have to," Paul said. "Why do you think they're fighting all the time?"

It was one thing to listen to Dad and Mom whispering. It was another to hear Paul's interpretation. "You don't know for sure," I said. "You keep the radio on."

"I don't have to hear everything to know," Paul said. "You know too. You just don't want to admit it."

"You don't think Dad's going to leave?" I said. "Not really?"

"I don't know," Paul said. "Maybe Mom'll kick him out. If Dad is having an affair, she shouldn't have to put up with it."

"They could get divorced?" I asked. "Dad could marry Lisa?"

"It's been known to happen," Paul said.

I started to cry.

"Don't worry," Paul said. "They might not get divorced. Mom might forgive him, or Dad might dump Lisa. Stranger things have happened."

"What about us?" I asked.

"We'll be okay," Paul said. "We'll keep living with Mom. If Dad does marry Lisa, they'll probably have a baby, but that's a long way off."

I could see that Paul had been thinking about it, and that scared me even more. Lots of times I'd

4

knocked on his door and he'd made fun of the things that frightened me. This time he didn't tell me how stupid I was. I'd kind of hoped he would. I tried hard to stop crying.

"There's no use worrying about it," Paul said. "Either it's going to happen or it isn't. They won't listen to us. Adults never do. You might as well just turn on the radio and act like nothing's happening."

"You won't go live with Dad?" I asked. "You'll stay with Mom and me?"

"Even if I wanted to go, Lisa wouldn't want me around," Paul said. "Besides, you and Mom need me."

"Thank you," I said.

Paul grinned. "You're welcome. Now get out of here and go to sleep. Mom and Dad'll still be married in the morning. Who knows? They might not even be whispering by then."

Paul was right. The next morning Mom and Dad were talking in normal voices. They weren't saying very much, and you could feel the anger between them like heat waves off summer pavement, but they weren't whispering. Neither one of them mentioned Lisa, and Paul and I sure didn't.

I walked to school thinking about Dad and Lisa. I used to take the school bus when I went to elementary school, but even though the schools were in a cluster, now that I was in middle school the bus didn't pick me up. Sometimes when it was raining Dad drove me to school and then went on to his office. Dad was a veterinarian, and Lisa was his receptionist. It seemed to me he could fire her and find a new receptionist pretty easily. Someone who wasn't twenty-five and pretty.

I was thinking about the whispers, about Dad and Lisa and Mom and Paul and me and divorce, all morning. It didn't matter too much in gym, what I was thinking about, or even in math, because I was lucky and my teacher didn't call on me. Third period was French, and I paid enough attention to get by.

But fourth period was English with Mrs. Erdman, and it was hard enough paying attention to her under normal circumstances, let alone when your parents were fighting and you were scared to death of a divorce. As Mrs. Erdman droned on, I stared out the window, trying to imagine what life would be like if Dad lived with Lisa. Would we move? Would Mom quit her job and start working someplace else? What if she couldn't get a job? Would Dad support us? Would they keep fighting? Would I have to spend every weekend at Dad's whether I had other plans or not? Would I have to be nice to Lisa knowing it was her fault my parents had split up?

I'd liked Lisa when she'd first started working for Dad, but that felt like a million years ago. If Dad married her, I'd never speak to her again. I wouldn't care if he was married to her for a hundred years and they had twenty babies.

Maybe Paul was wrong. Not about Dad and Lisa, but about what he and I could do. Maybe if I talked to Lisa, told her how happy we used to be, she'd realize she was doing something bad and she'd break off with Dad.

I could picture the whole scene. I'd go to Lisa's house and wait for her until she came home from work. Then I'd talk to her, woman to woman, about Mom and my family and how much we really meant to Dad.

Or maybe Dad would be there with her. He took Lisa home lots of times. I knew that from the whispers. I'd be waiting outside Lisa's house and Dad and Lisa would cross the street, laughing, the way he and Mom used to laugh, and then they'd see me.

Dad would be mad at first, because he'd think I was spying on him, but I'd tell him why I was there. Dad would stop being angry, he'd get quiet and thoughtful, and then he'd turn to Lisa and say I was right. He'd tell Lisa he was sorry, but she was just going to have to get another job. Then he'd give me a big hug and say, "Let's go home now, honey."

"Taryn! Taryn Powell!"

That wasn't Dad's voice. It wasn't even Lisa's. It was Mrs. Erdman's.

"Yes, Mrs. Erdman?" I said.

The whole class started laughing. They laughed even harder when Billy Fleming said, "Yes, Mrs. Erdman," just the way I had, soft and polite.

Mrs. Erdman's face was red and I could tell she was mad.

"Taryn, I asked you three times to come to the blackboard and correct this sentence. I might as well have been talking to a corpse!" Mrs. Erdman shouted.

"I am a corpse," Billy said. "I'm the living dead."

"Keep out of this, Billy, unless you want to be punished also!" Mrs. Erdman yelled. "I will not have my students ignoring me. Do you understand that?"

"Yes, Mrs. Erdman," I said. "I'm sorry. I was thinking about something important."

"Many of us have important things to think and worry about, but we have to do our jobs. Your job is to pay attention," Mrs. Erdman said. "Perhaps you'd care to share your thoughts with the class. Come up here, Taryn, and tell all of us what you were thinking."

"No," I said. "I mean, I can't."

"Get up here right now—or do I have to send you to the principal's office?" Mrs. Erdman said.

I stood up and walked to the front of the room. I could feel everyone's eyes on me. I tried to look at Nicole and Heather, my best friends, but they were looking at each other.

"Now tell the class exactly what you were thinking," Mrs. Erdman said. "We're all waiting breathlessly to learn what is so important to you, Taryn."

I stood there trying to get my mouth to work. There had to be something I could say. I'd known just what to say to my father in my daydream. Why was it so hard to find something to say in front of my English class?

The whole room was silent. I don't think I'd ever heard so much silence before. It was as if no one could even breathe until I managed to say something.

"I was thinking about sex," Billy said in that funny high-pitched voice. The whole class burst out laughing. Everyone except me. I kept standing there, only now I was crying. And Mrs. Erdman looked as if she didn't know who to kill first.

I couldn't bear standing there anymore, so I went back to my seat.

"I didn't tell you you could sit down," Mrs. Erdman said in a voice so cold everyone stopped laughing. "Get back up here, Taryn, and tell us what you were thinking about! And, class, if you make a single sound, it'll be detention for all of you for the rest of this week."

I went back to the front of the room, crying so hard that I didn't even try to look at Heather or Nicole.

"We're waiting, Taryn," Mrs. Erdman said firmly. "Tell us all what's so important."

I stood there, tears streaming down my cheeks, trying to stop. If my life had depended on it, I couldn't have said a word.

I stood there for what felt like hours. After a while the tears stopped, but I still couldn't talk. Mrs. Erdman kept me standing there until the bell rang for lunch. Then she dismissed everyone except Billy and me.

"I will not tolerate such behavior in my class," she said to us. "Billy, one more incident like the one today, and you'll have detention for the rest of the month. Do I make myself clear?"

"Yes, Mrs. Erdman," Billy said.

"You may go now," she said. Billy left.

"Now, Taryn," Mrs. Erdman began. "For me your lack of respect is the main problem here. Are you ready to share with me what was so important that you didn't hear me call your name three times?"

There was no one else in the room. If it had been any other teacher, I probably would have said I was worried about my parents. But I wasn't going to say that to Mrs. Erdman, especially not after what she'd done to me.

"I've forgotten," I said. "I'm sorry, Mrs. Erdman."

"Perhaps it will come back to you if you write all about it," Mrs. Erdman said. "I expect a thousand-word essay from you on my desk first thing tomorrow morning telling me exactly what was on your mind as you stared out the window and ignored me completely."

"A thousand words?" I said.

"That's four pages. And I'll be counting the words, so don't think you can get away with anything shorter. First thing tomorrow morning. Before the bell rings. And if it isn't there, I'll call your parents and tell them about your misbehavior."

"No, don't do that," I said. I realized at that moment how much I hated her. "I'll write it. I promise I will."

"Very well," Mrs. Erdman said. "You may leave now, Taryn."

Chapter Two

I went to the girls' room and cried in one of the stalls. Then I washed my face with cold water. For as long as I could remember, my mother had told me to wash my face with cold water after I'd cried. I wondered if Lisa knew stuff like that; then I told myself not to think about Lisa, at least not for the rest of the school day. She'd gotten me in enough trouble already.

When I got to the cafeteria, Heather and Nicole had saved me a seat. I was lucky to have two best friends, and even luckier that my two best friends were best friends with each other. Heather and Nicole were both Girl Scouts, and I wasn't, but Heather and I both loved to roller-skate, and Nicole didn't, and Nicole and I both took ballet lessons, and Heather didn't. So our friendship worked out perfectly.

"Are you okay?" Nicole asked.

"I wanted to kill Mrs. Erdman," Heather said.

"I wanted to kill Billy," Nicole said. "He only made it worse."

"Anyway, are you okay?" Heather asked. "We were worried when you didn't come down with us."

"I'm okay," I said. "I wanted to kill Mrs. Erdman and Billy too. And Billy and I were friends too, up until last summer. He used to be funny, not mean."

"Maybe he's taking meanness lessons from Mrs. Erdman," Nicole said.

"Mrs. Erdman's the meanest teacher I've ever had," Heather said. "I bet she's the meanest teacher ever. Remember how she picked on Lexi Richards last week?"

"And on Danny Jacobs," Nicole said. "I thought he was going to cry. And all he did was read the wrong sentence."

"Well, all Taryn did was not pay attention," Heather said. "No one ever pays attention to Mrs. Erdman anyway, she's so boring. I don't blame you, Taryn."

14

"Actually, it was kind of funny," Nicole said. "Mrs. Erdman called you three times and you could have been in another country the way you ignored her."

"What were you thinking about, anyway?" Heather said.

"Just stuff," I said, biting into the tuna sandwich Mom had packed for me. I hadn't told Heather and Nicole about the whispers yet. I couldn't imagine either of their fathers involved with a Lisa.

"It must have been pretty interesting stuff," Heather said. "I think a bomb could have gone off and you wouldn't have known."

"You're not so different," Nicole said. "Remember last week, in math class? You weren't paying attention when Mrs. Malloy called on you. Only she made a joke out of it. She just said, 'Earth to Heather,' instead of embarrassing you, the way Mrs. Erdman did to Taryn."

Heather giggled. "I was thinking about lunch," she admitted. "I didn't eat breakfast that morning, and by the time we had math all I could think about was food. Was that what you were thinking about, Taryn? Food?"

I nodded. "I was thinking about lunch too," I said.

"The two of you," Nicole said. "Breakfast is the most important meal of the day. Everyone says that. And now you know why."

"Because without it, teachers pick on you," Heather said. "Do you think that's why Mrs. Erdman is so mean? Because she doesn't eat enough breakfast?"

We all laughed. Mrs. Erdman was the fattest teacher in the school.

"That must be it," Nicole said. "She isn't getting enough nutrition."

"Her diet isn't balanced," Heather said. "Too many Twinkies, not enough protein."

"We should help her," Nicole said. "We should send her to a nutritionist."

"We should send her, all right," Heather said. "But not to a nutritionist."

It felt good to laugh with my friends. I even thought of telling them about Lisa, but I decided the school cafeteria wasn't the right place. We weren't exactly sitting alone. We were surrounded by other kids, and some of them had brothers and sisters in Paul's grade. I knew how fast a story could spread, so I kept my mouth shut.

"What did Mrs. Erdman say to you when she kept you after class?" Heather asked.

"She's making me write a thousand-word composition on what I was thinking about," I said. "And she said she'd count the words, so I can't cheat with big handwriting or anything."

"A thousand words?" Nicole repeated. "Boy, that sounds like a lot."

"And all of it about lunch," Heather said. "What are you eating, a tuna sandwich?"

I nodded.

"I don't think I could write a thousand words about a tuna sandwich," Heather said. "What can you say? Mayo or no mayo? Lettuce or no lettuce? Celery or no celery?"

"Definitely no celery," Nicole said. "I don't like celery."

"I don't think she's going to care what I write," I said. "Just as long as it's a thousand words."

"I don't know," Heather said. "If it's about food she might. We know how Mrs. Erdman loves her food."

"I bet she doesn't love celery," Nicole said. "Hot-fudge sundaes maybe, but not celery."

"Just like you, then," Heather said. "You don't like celery and you love hot-fudge sundaes. Maybe you'll grow up to look like Mrs. Erdman."

"I'd rather die," Nicole said. We all laughed,

because she sounded as if she really meant it. "What do you think Mr. Erdman looks like?"

"He's probably real skinny," Heather said. "He never has a chance to get to the food because Mrs. Erdman eats it all first."

"Poor Mr. Erdman," Nicole said. "He's stuck with Mrs. Erdman and he doesn't get enough to eat."

I'd started thinking about Lisa again. Maybe she fed Dad stuff Mom wouldn't let him eat. He was supposed to watch his cholesterol, and Mom was pretty strict about it. Dad loved pizza, but Mom had stopped getting it for us, even though some nights she came home from work too tired to cook.

Maybe Lisa lets Dad eat pizza, I thought. Maybe at work she calls the pizza place and they deliver extra-large pizza with Dad's favorite toppings. Pepperoni and sausage and extra cheese. Lisa probably let Dad eat whatever he wanted. I'd bet she encouraged him to do it because she didn't care about him the way Mom did. She was probably after Dad's money. She planned to marry him and let him eat all the pepperoni pizza he wanted. Then he'd die from too much cholesterol and she'd be his rich widow.

"No!" I said.

18

"What?" Heather said. "Taryn, what were you thinking about? I said your name twice and it was like you didn't hear me. And then you yelled out, 'No!'"

"She didn't exactly yell it," Nicole said. "Taryn, what's the matter? You can tell us."

But I couldn't. Not then and there, anyway. Instead I said, "I was thinking about Mrs. Erdman. And how much I hate her."

"It isn't fair," Heather said. "Teachers can be as mean as they want to kids, and kids have no way of getting back."

"There should be a way," I said. "There should be a way to get back at Mrs. Erdman and all the other grown-ups who are mean to kids."

"Like how?" Nicole asked. "Remember, it has to be legal."

I thought about it for a minute. I thought about how much I hated Mrs. Erdman and Lisa. I had no way of stopping either of them. I was just a kid, and kids couldn't do anything to grown-ups, no matter how cruel the grown-ups were. Kids just had to accept it.

I thought about turning the other cheek and how you were supposed to forgive and forget, but none of that made me feel any better. If Mrs. Erdman

19

had died right in front of me that very moment, I wouldn't have cared. And if Lisa had died the same way, I'd have felt glad.

"You'd think there'd be a way," Heather said. "Some kind of joke, maybe, you could pull."

I smiled because I'd figured out what to do. "The idea isn't to be mean to Mrs. Erdman," I said.

"It isn't?" Heather asked.

I shook my head. "It's to be nice to *Mr.* Erdman," I said. "Poor hungry Mr. Erdman."

"How?" Nicole said.

"Well, we agree he doesn't have enough to eat," I said. "Because Mrs. Erdman hogs all the food. So we have to make sure he gets something to eat."

"You mean we should bring him something like cookies?" Heather asked. "And not let Mrs. Erdman eat any of them?"

"How could we manage that?" Nicole asked. "Mrs. Erdman would probably steal them from him. I bet she'd steal candy from a baby if she had a chance."

"We have to see to it that there's so much food even Mr. Erdman can get some," I explained. "Like ordering an extra-large pizza for just the two of them."

"Maybe Mrs. Erdman has kids," Heather said.

"She couldn't," Nicole said. "She would have eaten them at birth."

"Ooh, that's disgusting," Heather said, but we laughed anyway. "I still don't think one pizza would be enough."

"You're right," I said. "We should order more. Lots more. A half dozen pizzas, extra-large. Five for Mrs. Erdman and one for poor Mr. Erdman."

"With everything on them," Heather said.

"Including anchovies?" Nicole asked. "I hate anchovies."

"Lots of anchovies," I said. "And pepperoni and sausage and extra cheese."

"That would cost a fortune," Heather said. "How could we pay for something like that?"

"We wouldn't pay," I said. "We'd have them delivered to Mrs. Erdman's house. She'd have to pay for them."

"That's only fair, since she'd eat most of them," Nicole said.

"It's almost like a good deed," Heather said. "Seeing to it that poor Mr. Erdman has enough to eat at least one day of his life."

"Poor Mr. Erdman," Nicole said. "I sure hope he likes anchovies."

"It would be so easy," I said. "All you'd have

to do is call a pizza place and order them. Then Mrs. Erdman would get the delivery and she'd have to pay for six extra-large pizzas with everything on them.''

"I think one of them should be plain," Nicole said. "In case poor Mr. Erdman doesn't like anchovies or something."

"Okay," I said. "One plain and all the rest with everything on them. And they'd never know who ordered the pizzas."

"That's for the best," Heather said. "Acts of true generosity are best when they're anonymous."

I started to think about sending the pizzas to Lisa. She could get a half dozen pizzas every day until she realized what was happening and how miserable her life would be unless she gave Dad up.

"I'll look up her address in the phone book," I said. "It'll be easy."

"Whose address?" Nicole asked.

"Mrs. Erdman," I said. "I could look her address up in the phone book."

Heather gave me a look. "You're not really going to do it, are you, Taryn? Order all those pizzas for Mrs. Erdman?"

"Oh, no, of course not," I said, and looked at Heather. "I would *never* do that." And I knew I wouldn't, either, no matter how much I hated Mrs. Erdman. Because my real enemy was Lisa, and I was going to save all my best ideas for her.

Chapter Three

The public library is a couple of blocks from school. It seemed the easiest place for me to do my research.

The first thing you saw when you walked into the library were three pay phones. They were on the wall to your left as you faced the main door. But when I went over to them I realized there weren't any phone books. I had to go to the main desk and ask.

"You'll find them at Reference," the librarian told me. She pointed to the reference desk, and I walked over.

"May I help you?" the reference librarian

asked. "I know you. You're Dr. Powell's daughter, aren't you?"

"Yes, I am," I answered politely.

"Dr. Powell is my dog's vet," she said. "Your dad is wonderful. Half the staff here take their pets to him."

"Thank you," I said, wondering how the staff would feel if they knew about my dad and his receptionist.

"Please give him my regards," the librarian said. "Tell him Branwell's mother says hello. He often jokes that my dog is the only Branwell he knows."

"Branwell," I said. "I'll do that."

The librarian looked at me as if I was someone special. "Now how can I help you?" she asked.

"I need a phone book," I said. "That's all."

I thought the librarian gave me a funny look, as if she thought I was up to something. "A local one?" she asked. "Or one for someplace else?"

"Local," I said calmly.

She went behind the desk and pulled out a phone book. "Here it is," she said. "Please look up your number on the desk here. We have more people tearing pages out of phone books instead of copying down what they need. We have to keep an eagle eye on them.''

''I'm not going to do that,'' I said.

''I know you aren't,'' the librarian said. ''It's just the rule we have to follow.''

It made me feel funny to have her staring at me, as if she knew I was going to do something bad. Maybe that was why, instead of starting with Lisa's number, I looked up *Erdman* first.

There it was. *Erdman, Mr. and Mrs. Henry. 117 Elm Blvd. 555-2222.*

It was funny seeing her name like that, as if she was a normal person and not a teacher. Poor Mr. Erdman, I thought. Mr. Skinny Henry Erdman, stuck married to such a horrible person.

I didn't know if the librarian was still watching me, but I looked up my own family next. There we were, the Powells of Harmony Drive.

Lisa came next. What was her last name? It was something easy, but I had to concentrate to remember it. I knew it, but it made me nervous to have that librarian in front of me.

Brown! Lisa Brown. That was it.

I turned to the front of the phone book and found the listings for *Brown*. There were a lot of them, and there were other listings under *Browne*.

Lisa was not in the phone book. Not a single Lisa Brown or Lisa Browne.

I nearly cried. I knew it was dumb, but I couldn't think of any other way to keep Mom and Dad together. And it felt wrong somehow that Dad was so involved with Lisa and I couldn't even find her phone number. What if I needed it someday in an emergency?

I looked at the phone book more carefully and found three listings for *L. Brown* and one for *L. Browne.*

Any one of them could be Lisa. Mom had once told me that sometimes women who lived alone listed themselves by their first initial.

Three L. Browns and one L. Browne. Which one was Lisa?

I looked at the addresses. The first L. Brown lived on Harding Drive, and I didn't know where that was. The second one lived on Westhaven Avenue, which was within walking distance of the library. The third lived on Sycamore Lane, toward the other end of town, near Elm Boulevard, where Mrs. Erdman lived. And L. Browne lived on South Second Street, also within walking distance of the library.

"I need to copy these down," I said to the librarian. "It's for a report I'm doing."

"Certainly," she said. She gave me a piece of paper and a pencil.

I wrote down all four addresses and also the phone numbers just in case, and I closed the book and gave it back. "Thank you. I'm sorry if I took too much time," I said.

"Not at all," she answered. "And remember, tell Dr. Powell that Branwell's mother said hi."

"Okay," I said. I walked toward the telephones. If Lisa had an answering machine, I'd know which L. Brown was her just by calling.

I reached into my pocket to find some change. All I had was one quarter. I could call one of them, and I'd have a one-in-four chance of getting the right one. Assuming Lisa had an answering machine.

Which one to pick? I decided to call the L. Brown who lived nearest Dad's office. I stared at the paper. What if Lisa was in? She should be at the office, but maybe she was home sick. Or maybe Dad had given her the afternoon off to go shopping or something. What would I say if I heard her voice over the phone?

I decided not to say anything, just in case she recognized my voice. People call and hang up all the time. Lisa would never know it was me. Even if she did figure it out, that was okay too. I wanted her to know she had an enemy.

I looked at the paper again and again, put the quarter in the phone, and punched in L. Brown's number.

After four rings someone picked up. "You have reached 555-2723," a woman's voice said. "Please leave your message after the beep."

I hung up. Was it Lisa's voice? I thought it might be, but I wasn't sure. Suddenly I felt as if I absolutely had to know if it was Lisa's voice, if she was the L. Brown who lived at 447 Westhaven Avenue.

The one thing I knew about this L. Brown was that she wasn't at home. I could go there and wait—actually, hide, until she came home from work. And if it was Lisa, I'd see her and I'd know her phone number and address.

The more I thought about it, the more I liked the idea.

I picked up my book bag and left the library. I knew there was a chance that L. Brown of Westhaven Avenue wasn't Lisa, but the more I thought about it, the more convinced I was that I'd found the right one. And with a little patience, it would be easy for me to find out for sure.

"Oh, no," I said when I found 447 Westhaven. It was a six-story apartment building.

I'd been sure Lisa lived in a house. I'd pictured myself hiding behind a tree, waiting for her to drive up. Now I had to find her in an apartment building.

I tried to remember everything I knew about Lisa and realized it was next to nothing. She was young. She was pretty. She knew how to answer the phones and do the paperwork. She had problems of some sort, according to Dad. The first thing that got Mom upset and started the whispering was when Dad started to help Lisa with her problems.

I walked over to the door of the apartment building and stood there for a minute or two, trying to figure out what to do. The list next to the buzzers said L. Brown lived in 3A.

An older woman walked to the door carrying two bags of groceries while struggling to get her keys out.

"If you'd like, I'll hold your bags for you," I offered.

"Thank you," the woman said, looking me up and down.

I took the bags from her. They didn't weigh very

much. The lady opened her purse, found her keys, and unlocked the front door.

"Would you like me to carry these in for you?" I asked. "I was on my way in anyway."

"That's very sweet of you," she said. She looked kind of like my great-grandmother. The two of us walked into 447 Westhaven Avenue together, and I followed her into the elevator. She pressed 4.

"Do you live in the building?" she asked. "I don't think I recognize you."

"I'm here to visit my aunt," I said. I don't know why I said that instead of saying I was there to play with a friend, except I didn't know how many kids there were in 447 and there had to be plenty of people who could be my aunt. I was glad when the lady didn't ask me any more questions. I guessed I looked trustworthy.

We got out on the fourth floor, and I walked her to her apartment. "Let me give you something for all your help," she said, reaching for her change purse.

"Oh, no, you don't have to," I said. "I was coming in anyway."

"You're a very sweet girl," she said. "Your parents must be very proud of you."

"Thank you," I said, then went back to the elevator. I pressed 3 and got off. There was no one else on the floor. I walked to apartment 3A and rang the bell. My heart pounded like crazy, but nobody answered.

I needed a place to hide. I found the stairwell. If I kept the door open a crack, I had a good view of the elevator and an okay one of 3A.

It was nearly four o'clock. Dad closed the office at four-thirty. If Lisa went straight home from work, she'd be at 447 Westhaven by five-fifteen. If she didn't . . . well, I couldn't bear that thought.

I took out my math book and started my homework. When you're hiding in a stairwell, even math is a welcome distraction. When I finished my math, I pretended I was a cop on a stakeout. But that seemed kind of childish, so I stopped pretending and read my social studies instead.

Twice the elevator stopped on the third floor. Both times I put my books down quietly and peeked out. The first time, a man got off. The second time, it was a young woman, and for a second I was sure it was Lisa.

I began to worry that maybe I'd read the numbers wrong and 3A wasn't where I thought it was. Just to be sure, I left the stairwell and went back to the door of 3A. It was just where I'd left it. I tiptoed to the stairwell and continued hiding.

Four-thirty came and went. Four-forty-five. I told myself that was good, it was too early for her to get back. Everything was right on schedule.

But when five o'clock came and Lisa still hadn't shown up, I got discouraged, even though she really wasn't due till five-fifteen. I didn't know how detectives could sit around waiting for people all day. They didn't even have math homework to do while they were waiting.

At 5:17 the elevator stopped on the third floor. As the door opened, I practically stopped breathing. I stuck my head out as little as possible and saw the back of a woman who was walking away from the elevator.

It could be Lisa, I thought. She walked to apartment 3A and stopped. I gasped, hoping the woman wouldn't hear me. She took out her key and unlocked 3A.

Suddenly she turned her head in my direction and I could see her face.

It wasn't Lisa. I'd spent all that time in the stairwell only to find that L. Brown of 447 Westhaven Avenue wasn't the Lisa Brown I was looking for.

Chapter Four

The next morning, on my way to school, I remembered the thousand-word composition I was supposed to give to Mrs. Erdman.

I just about died. I stood absolutely still on Prospect Street and thought I would collapse on the sidewalk. I had never been so scared in all my life.

It wasn't as if I'd meant to forget. It was just that finding Lisa Brown had been so important to me, and then there had been all that waiting (when I could have been writing the composition if I'd only remembered), and then I'd gone home and had to make up a story about where I'd been all afternoon (at the library, I'd said, because at least that was a little bit true), and then since I'd done all my homework Mom let me watch TV all evening. I'd fallen asleep to the whispers and the next thing I knew Mom was telling me it was time to get up. I had totally forgotten about the composition.

I started feeling mad at Mrs. Erdman for giving me that assignment. I wasn't about to tell her what I'd really been thinking. It made me feel dirty imagining her reading about Mom and Dad. Still, I was in real trouble. Mrs. Erdman wasn't going to accept the idea that I'd simply forgotten. She'd report me to the principal, and the principal would call in my parents. Then the whispers would turn into screams and things would be said that I never wanted to hear.

I stood there on Prospect Street trying to decide what to do. I'm smart, I told myself. I figured out how to find Lisa Brown. I might not have found the right one, but I'd solved the problem. On my report card the year before one of my teachers had written that I was very good at solving problems. This was my chance to prove it.

I'll run away, I decided. Not forever, just for a day or two. Just long enough for everybody to worry about me. Maybe Heather or Nicole would tell my parents about Mrs. Erdman and they'd get mad at her and get her fired. Mom and Dad would realize they were responsible for my running away, and Dad would fire Lisa. Then he and Mom would be happy again. I'd come home, looking sad and thin, and everybody would tell me how much they loved me and how sorry they were for everything. Even Mrs. Erdman would apologize, but she'd still stay fired.

I loved it. The only problem was the running away part. I wasn't sure where a twelve-year-old girl with a couple of dollars on her could go. I wasn't about to hitch a ride with a stranger, and I couldn't see walking someplace really far away. I'd gotten tired walking to Westhaven Avenue the day before, and that wasn't even the other end of town.

The truth was, I wasn't brave enough or scared enough to run away.

I thought about cutting school, but that wasn't such a hot idea either.

Finally I came up with a solution. I'd get to school just as the bell was ringing so that I wouldn't have time to bring the composition to Mrs. Erdman's room. Instead I'd write it during math and French and give it to her at the start of English. It would be hard to write and pay attention during classes, but it was the best I could come up with.

So I kind of hid until the last moment. I didn't want to talk to anybody anyway. I'd been getting pretty good at hiding lately. This time I didn't even need a stairwell.

As soon as I heard the school bell ring, I started to run. I made it inside the building right as the last bell rang.

The second I got to homeroom, Mrs. Jenkins, my homeroom teacher, told me to go to the principal's office. I couldn't believe it. Mrs. Erdman had reported me already. I knew I should have run away.

I walked to the principal's office, trying to make up my mind what to do. I finally decided to tell her the truth. Our principal was Mrs. Delmonico, and I liked her. I'd never been in trouble before, so I didn't know how she'd react, but at that point it just seemed easier to admit I had forgotten to write the composition. I'd tell her I'd been thinking about my parents because there was a family problem. I didn't think she'd make me tell what the problem was, especially when I'd start crying, which I was one hundred percent sure I would do. She'd probably call Mom and Dad, but that was okay too. It was time they knew that I heard them whispering.

It all sounded fine until I got to the main office. Then I began to shake. I was shaking so hard that I didn't think I'd be able to open my mouth. "I'm Taryn Powell," I said softly to Ms. Schultz, the school secretary.

"In there, Taryn," Ms. Schultz said, pointing to the principal's office. She looked really upset. I couldn't believe it was such a big deal that I hadn't handed in the composition yet. How did all these people know I hadn't written it?

I walked into Mrs. Delmonico's office and saw her sitting at her desk. The room was full of other kids. All girls, I realized, and then I saw they were all girls from my class. Heather and Nicole were there, and Jennifer Margolis and Kareema Johnson and Lexi Richards. The room was totally quiet.

"I'm Taryn Powell," I said. "Mrs. Jenkins sent me here."

"Yes, Taryn," Mrs. Delmonico said. "We've been waiting for you. Taryn, where did you go after school yesterday?"

"What?" I said. Had Mrs. Delmonico found out I was trying to spy on Lisa? And if she had, what were the other girls doing there? What was going on?

"After school yesterday," Mrs. Delmonico said. "Where did you go?"

"To the library," I said, because it was sort of the truth and because it was the same half-lie I'd told my parents the day before.

"I told you," Lexi Richards said. "Taryn and I were at the library together until almost six. Right, Taryn?"

"Right," I said, because I had no idea what I'd gotten into, but I knew that lie was my lifeline. "Then I went home for supper."

"Taryn, will you swear that you didn't leave Lexi to make a phone call around four-thirty yesterday afternoon?" Mrs. Delmonico asked.

I knew exactly where I'd been at four-thirty and it wasn't near any telephones. The part about Lexi was a lie, but the rest of it was true enough. "I didn't call anyone at four-thirty," I said. "Who was I supposed to have called?"

"It's the pizzas," Heather said.

"What pizzas?" I asked.

"Yesterday at four-thirty, someone called in an order of a half dozen pizzas with everything on them to be delivered to Mrs. Erdman's house," Mrs. Delmonico said. "Several students said they heard you talking about doing that at lunch yesterday. Is that true, Taryn?"

"I guess," I said. "But I didn't do it. It was just a joke."

"Well, it was a costly and unpleasant joke," Mrs. Delmonico said. "The bill for the pizzas came to nearly a hundred dollars. They were delivered to Mrs. Erdman's house, where Mr. Erdman is recuperating from triple-bypass heart surgery. He's on a severely restricted diet and it was very upsetting to him and to Mrs. Erdman to have those pizzas brought to their home. Mrs. Erdman was so upset that she took today off from school."

"I didn't do it," I said. "Honestly."

Mrs. Delmonico looked at me. "Girls, you can all leave now," she said. "Except for Taryn and Lexi."

The other girls left the room. Heather and Nicole gave me looks as if they were at my funeral. I kind of wished they were.

Lexi was standing at the far end of Mrs. Delmonico's desk. I edged closer to her.

"Taryn, Lexi says you met at the library yesterday afternoon," Mrs. Delmonico said. "She says she saw you at the reference desk and waved you over and the two of you stayed together for the rest of the afternoon."

"That's what I said," Lexi said. "We did our

homework together and we talked. But only in whispers, like you're supposed to at the library.''

"Did you ever leave Lexi during that time?'' Mrs. Delmonico asked. "To go to the bathroom or for any other reason?''

Every nerve in my body was screaming. All I wanted to do was bolt out of that room. But I couldn't, because if I did, Mrs. Delmonico would be sure I was the one who'd ordered those pizzas.

"After I left the reference desk, I used the phone in the lobby,'' I said truthfully. "But that was nowhere near four-thirty. And I didn't call any pizza place.''

"Who did you call?'' Mrs. Delmonico asked.

Truth time was over. "I called home,'' I said. "I wanted them to know I was going to be at the library. I figured since I was going to be there with Lexi, I might be late.''

"Who did you speak to?'' Mrs. Delmonico asked.

"I didn't speak to anybody,'' I said. "No one was home. I left a message. But that was closer to three-thirty than four-thirty.''

"Much closer,'' Lexi said.

"And then you joined Lexi?'' Mrs. Delmonico asked me.

I wished I knew better what Lexi had said. All I could do was nod.

"Are you and Lexi close friends?" Mrs. Delmonico asked.

"No," I said. "I'm sorry, Lexi, but we aren't."

"I know," Lexi said. "I told Mrs. Delmonico the same thing. That was why I was so happy when we spent yesterday afternoon together. Because I like you, but we aren't really friends."

"But you do admit, Taryn, that ordering those pizzas was your idea," Mrs. Delmonico said.

"Yes, ma'am," I said.

"And, Lexi, did you hear Taryn make that suggestion?" Mrs. Delmonico asked. "About ordering the pizzas?"

"I did," Lexi said. "But so did lots of other kids. Taryn wasn't exactly whispering."

"Lexi, you can go now," Mrs. Delmonico said. "Ask Ms. Schultz for a late pass."

Lexi left.

"Sit down, Taryn," Mrs. Delmonico said. I did. "Now tell me again exactly what you did when you left school yesterday."

"I went to the library," I said. "I went to the reference desk. I saw Lexi. I made a phone call home. I went over to Lexi and we did our homework together. Then I went home."

"And you didn't leave her side?" Mrs. Delmonico asked.

"No, ma'am, I didn't," I said. "Not until I left for home, and that was after five-thirty." By this time the story was feeling so familiar to me that I almost believed it myself. And I liked it a lot more than the truth about hiding in a stairwell waiting for L. Brown to show up so that I could be sure it was really my father's girlfriend's address when I called up a pizza place to have them deliver a half dozen pizzas to her home.

"But you admit sending the pizzas was your idea," Mrs. Delmonico said.

I nodded.

"And who did you tell that idea to?" Mrs. Delmonico asked.

"Heather and Nicole," I said. "But we were all joking. They wouldn't have done it."

"They were at a Girl Scout meeting yesterday afternoon," Mrs. Delmonico said. "With my daughter, as a matter of fact. I know neither of them did it."

I was glad for Heather and Nicole but annoyed at the same time. They were my best friends, and they should have defended me. Heather and Nicole knew me so well. The three of us had met in kindergarten and had become close right away. Until today I'd thought we would always stick together, even if they were at a Girl Scout meeting while I was hiding in a stairwell.

"If you didn't order those pizzas, do you have any idea who did?" Mrs. Delmonico asked.

I shook my head.

"Was Mrs. Erdman ever mean to Lexi?" Mrs. Delmonico asked.

"Mrs. Erdman's been mean to most of us," I said.

"And what did she do that made you so angry at her?" Mrs. Delmonico asked.

It was funny. Yesterday morning it had seemed like the most important thing in my life. Standing in front of the class like that. Everyone laughing at me. Now I could hardly remember. "I wasn't paying attention," I said. "And she asked me what I was thinking about, only I couldn't tell her. So she made me stand in front of the class."

"And that's why you were so angry with her?" Mrs. Delmonico asked.

"I was crying," I said. "And she wouldn't let me sit down. And nobody likes her. She's mean to everybody, not just me. I came up with the idea for the pizzas, but I didn't send them. I don't know who did, and I don't even care. I'm sorry about her husband, but she's a mean teacher, and somebody was mad enough at her to order those pizzas. It wasn't me and it wasn't Heather or Nicole or Lexi either. There were lots of kids who could have heard me talking at lunch, and there are lots of kids who don't like Mrs. Erdman.''

"I'm going to find out who did this," Mrs. Delmonico said. "The pizza place is owed a great deal of money, and Mrs. Erdman is quite upset. It was your idea, Taryn, and even though you and Lexi tell the same story, I still have to regard you as the most likely culprit.''

"I didn't do it!" I said.

"I only wish I could be sure," Mrs. Delmonico said. "Very well, Taryn. Go to your class. But keep in mind that until I learn who sent those pizzas, I will have to assume you were involved.''

Chapter Five

Have you ever had to go to the bathroom really bad but for some reason you can't get to one? It makes you go crazy.

That's pretty much how I felt all day. I desperately wanted to talk to Heather and Nicole and especially to Lexi Richards, but I knew I couldn't at school. It felt as if everyone was looking at me, waiting for me to confess. I couldn't take the chance that anyone would overhear.

At lunchtime Heather, Nicole, and I did our share of whispering. It was the first real chance we had to talk, and I was glad because it made me realize that we were still best friends. I only wished we had more privacy. I couldn't say everything I wanted, but just being with Heather and Nicole made me feel better.

"All the girls were called into Mrs. Delmonico's office," Nicole said. "When Mrs. Erdman called the pizza place back, the guy said he'd talked to a girl."

"Then Mrs. Delmonico asked if any of us had done it, so of course we said no," Heather said. "But Sarah Weatherby looked kind of funny, and she said she had heard something about pizzas at lunch."

"Then Tiffany said she had too. She wasn't sure who said it exactly, but she thought maybe it was me," Nicole said. "And I thought Tiffany was my friend."

"So naturally Nicole said she hadn't said anything like that, and even if she had, she would never order pizzas just to play a practical joke," Heather said.

"But Mrs. Delmonico asked some of the other girls if they thought I'd been the one talking about pizzas, and a couple of them said yes," Nicole said.

"And Maryanne said she remembered hearing me saying something about pizzas too," Heather said.

"So Heather got real upset," Nicole said. "And

she kind of said something about how it was your idea.''

"But I said right away I was sure you didn't have anything to do with it,'' Heather declared. ''You didn't, did you, Taryn?''

"No,'' I said. ''I didn't.''

"See, I told you,'' Heather said to Nicole. ''I knew you were innocent, Taryn.''

"You mean you thought I did it?'' I asked Nicole, and my voice got a little louder, the way Mom's did when she said Lisa's name.

Nicole blushed. ''I didn't think you did,'' she said. ''But I didn't know who else would have. And you were so mad at Mrs. Erdman yesterday, I thought, well, maybe.''

"But she didn't say you did,'' Heather said. ''She just said to Mrs. Delmonico that you'd been joking about it at lunch yesterday.''

"But Maryanne said you'd been crying,'' Nicole said. ''And some of the other girls said Mrs. Erdman had made you cry.''

"Then Mrs. Delmonico asked who'd been sitting where at lunch,'' Heather said. ''When we figured it out, Mrs. Delmonico dismissed most of the girls and kept the ones who were sitting nearest to you.''

"It was so weird that you weren't there yet,''

Nicole said. "Like you'd run away or something. We all kept waiting for you."

"And while we were waiting Mrs. Delmonico asked us if any of us had seen you after school yesterday," Heather said. "And Lexi said she ran into you at the library and the two of you spent the afternoon together."

"You never told me you and Lexi were friends," Nicole said.

"We're not," I said.

"Then it was a lucky thing you ran into her," Heather said. "Once Mrs. Delmonico told us what time the pizzas had been ordered, I knew she couldn't blame Nicole or me, because we'd been at our Girl Scout meeting. So what did you tell Mrs. Delmonico when we left?"

"I told her I didn't do it," I said.

"Well, I hope she believes you," Nicole said. "You and Lexi were really together the whole time?"

"Yes, we were," I said, and my voice got loud again. I wasn't used to lying, and I blushed again, but it didn't matter. I wasn't even sure it mattered that my two best friends thought I might have played such a mean joke. And I couldn't really blame them. After all, I had meant to. Just not on Mrs. Erdman.

At the end of the school day, I found Lexi at her locker and whispered, "We have to talk."

Lexi just nodded. She was an even bigger liar than me, so I guess she had more experience with keeping quiet.

She left school first, and I followed her. When we were a couple of blocks away she stopped walking and waited for me.

"Boy, was I relieved when you said you'd gone to the library," she said. "I was so afraid you'd make up a story because you were scared."

"How did you know I went to the library?" I asked.

"I saw you there," Lexi said. "Just like I told Mrs. Delmonico. I saw you at the reference desk and I waved at you but you didn't see me."

"I'm sorry," I said.

"That's okay," Lexi said. "Lots of people don't see me. I'm used to it."

I looked at her then. Lexi was one of the smaller girls in seventh grade. She'd moved to our town near the end of the past year, so she wasn't exactly a new girl, but I didn't know her well enough to like or dislike her. I did know that if I'd seen her waving to me at the library I would have ignored her. And that made me feel bad.

"I'm sorry," I said again.

"Oh, don't be," Lexi said. "It's okay that nobody notices me."

"But why did you say that I saw you?" I asked. "Why did you lie?"

"Because I like you," Lexi said. "You've always been nice to me."

"I have?" I said.

"Well, nicer than a lot of the other kids," Lexi said. "And I wanted us to be friends. Besides, I hate Mrs. Erdman, and I didn't care who sent her all those pizzas. She made me cry last week, and I hated it when she made you cry yesterday. And everybody was blaming you and you weren't there to defend yourself. It made me so mad. So I said you and I spent the afternoon together. Like I'd hoped we would when I saw you at the library and waved. I kind of waved like this." She gave her right hand a little shake. "Maybe I should learn to wave bigger. Maybe that's why nobody ever notices me."

"I had a lot of stuff on my mind," I said. "You could have waved like this"—I stretched my arms over my head and waved them wildly—"and I still wouldn't have noticed."

"I could see you were worried about something," Lexi said. "I kind of watched you, hoping you'd notice. I saw you looking through the telephone book."

I remembered how I'd found Mrs. Erdman's address and phone number. I must have set the world's record for blushing. "I didn't order those pizzas," I said.

"I don't care," Lexi said.

"I didn't," I said. I just wanted one person to believe me.

Lexi gave me a long, hard look. "All right," she said. "You didn't order the pizzas. I believe you."

"Do you really?" I asked.

She nodded.

"I'd tell you where I was, but I can't," I said.

"Okay," she said.

I looked at her then and thought there was no reason not to tell her. Here she was, someone who hardly knew me, and she was showing more faith in me than either of my best friends.

"I was spying," I said. "At least, I was trying to."

"On who?" Lexi asked.

"I think my father has a girlfriend," I said. It felt so strange hearing those words come out of my mouth. "And I was looking for her."

"But you didn't find her?" Lexi asked.

"I went to the wrong apartment," I said. "That's why I was reading the phone book yesterday. Trying to find her address. Only there were four people with her name and I didn't know which one she was, and I went to the wrong place. You do believe me, don't you?"

Lexi nodded. "My parents are divorced," she said. "That's why we moved last year. My mom and me. Dad had lots of girlfriends. Mom says she put up with it for as long as she could and then she decided to leave him. Dad's an airplane pilot. We used to live in a nice house, only now we live in an apartment. It's okay, but I miss the house where we used to live. I've only seen my dad once since we moved. He's always so busy. I spent a weekend with him last summer, but he was real busy the whole time. He wasn't flying, but he was busy anyway, with his newest girlfriend. She tried to be nice to me, but I could see she didn't want me around. Neither did Dad. He hasn't asked me back."

"That's terrible," I said.

Lexi nodded. "But it'll be okay. That's what Mom keeps telling me. I'll make friends and like it here. And it's nice not hearing them fight all the time. Once I make friends I know I'll be happy."

"I hope that's real soon," I said.

"Do you think your parents are going to get a divorce?" Lexi asked.

"I'm not sure," I said. "They fight in whispers."

"My parents screamed," Lexi said. "Maybe it's better if it's whispers. Maybe that means they're not so mad at each other."

"I hope so," I said. "But it's scary anyway."

"I know," Lexi said. "When Mrs. Erdman picked on you, you were thinking about your parents, weren't you?"

"Yes," I answered.

"I thought about my parents a lot when they were fighting. My grades went down and everything," Lexi said. "Teachers are supposed to care about that stuff, but I don't think they do. Well, some of them maybe, but most of them are just too busy."

"Or too mean," I said. "Like Mrs. Erdman."

"She's the meanest teacher I ever saw," Lexi said. "She belongs in the record books."

I laughed. It felt good to laugh. Lexi laughed with me. We stood on the sidewalk and laughed for a long time.

"Mrs. Delmonico still thinks I did it," I said once we calmed down. "And there's no way I can prove to her I didn't."

"Sure there is," Lexi said. "I spent a lot of today thinking about it."

"How?" I asked. "I can't tell her the truth, because I don't have any witnesses. And even if she believed me she'd realize we were both lying."

"There is another way," Lexi said. "All we have to do is find the girl who really ordered the pizzas and then you can clear your name."

"Like detectives," I said.

"Exactly," Lexi said. "You and me. We'll figure out who did it and get her to admit it, and then no one will care where you were when the pizzas were ordered."

I smiled at Lexi. Neither Heather nor Nicole had offered to help me find out who really was guilty. Only Lexi had. And it was Lexi who had lied for me. Lexi who believed in me.

"Partners," I said, and held out my hand.

Lexi smiled as if she'd just won the lottery. She shook my hand and said, "Partners."

Chapter Six

"Now what do we do?" Lexi said.

"I don't know," I said.

"Neither do I," Lexi said, and we both started laughing.

"We need a plan," I said.

"A good plan," Lexi said, and we practically fell on the sidewalk, we were laughing so hard.

"I'm sorry," Lexi said once we were both calm. "I get hysterical sometimes when I'm nervous."

"Me too," I said. "This has just been the worst couple of days."

"I bet," Lexi said.

"Things will get better when they know I'm innocent," I said. "They'll be better for you too, since you won't have to keep covering for me."

"I don't mind," Lexi said. "I don't want you to get in trouble for something you didn't do."

"I'm already in trouble," I said. "And as long as they think I really did order the pizzas, they're going to think you're involved too. So we have to find out who did it. That way you'll be cleared as well as me."

Lexi nodded. "Do you have any idea who might have done it?" she asked.

"No. But it had to be somebody who doesn't like Mrs. Erdman."

"But nobody likes her," Lexi pointed out. "That leaves our whole class."

"Maybe not," I said. "We know it was a girl who called. And we know Heather and Nicole couldn't have done it. I bet some of the other girls have alibis too."

"And . . . ," Lexi said, but then she looked away from me.

"And what?" I asked.

"It had to be somebody who heard you come up with the idea," she said. "It's too weird a coincidence that some girl did it the same day you joked about it."

"Yeah," I said. I understood why Lexi hadn't wanted to say it. It didn't make me feel any better knowing I'd given somebody the idea for such a mean trick.

"I was nearby," Lexi said. "I heard a lot of what you were talking about."

"But we know you didn't do it either," I said. "Do you remember who else was near me?"

"Kareema and Jennifer," Lexi said. "But they were mostly talking to each other."

"Heather and Nicole said Maryanne and Tiffany and Sarah all heard too," I said. "Half the girls in seventh grade must have heard me."

"You *were* talking kind of loud," Lexi said. "We all knew how upset you were."

I sighed. "I guess we could ask all of them where they were yesterday at four-thirty. Maybe they all have alibis except one."

"Do you really think so?" Lexi asked.

"No," I said. "Besides, they could lie. I'm lying about my alibi, after all. And I lied to the principal. It's a lot easier to lie to a kid."

Lexi scrunched up her face. I guessed that meant she was thinking. "Maybe we're doing this the wrong way," she said. "We want to clear your name, right?"

"Right," I said.

"Well, there are two ways to do that. We can find out who's guilty or we can prove you're innocent."

"But how can we prove I'm innocent unless we find out who's guilty?" I asked.

"That's the hard part," Lexi admitted. "I haven't solved that yet."

We just stood there thinking about it.

"The pizza place," I said. "If we can find the pizza place, maybe they'll know it wasn't my voice."

"Sure," Lexi said. "Kids sound different from each other, the same as grown-ups."

"At least it's worth a try," I said. "How many pizza places do you think there are here?"

"Thousands," Lexi said. "My mom says this must be the pizza capital of the universe."

I refused to be discouraged. "Most of them don't deliver," I said. "We can eliminate all the ones that don't."

"Let's walk up and down Central Avenue," Lexi said. "We can stop off at the pizza places there. Maybe we'll be lucky and find the right one."

I nodded. Central Avenue was only a couple of blocks away. It was the main street in town, and it had lots of restaurants.

"This is a smart way to do it," Lexi said. "If we

find the right place and they say it wasn't you, then you'll clear your name nice and easy."

"And if we don't find the pizza place on Central Avenue, I'll call all the other places," I said. "Sooner or later I'll find the right one. And since I wasn't the one who made the call, they're bound to clear me."

"Then it won't matter who did it," Lexi said. "You know, if they hadn't said you did it I wouldn't care who did. I really hate Mrs. Erdman. I don't care if her husband is recovering from surgery and all that."

"Well, it was mean," I said. "I would have never done it to my father's girlfriend if I knew her husband was recovering from heart surgery."

"Is she married?" Lexi asked. "Your father's girlfriend, I mean."

"No," I said. "But if she was, I wouldn't. Oh, you know what I mean."

"Yes, I do," Lexi said.

I smiled. I couldn't help it. Even though I was in a whole lot of trouble, I was starting to enjoy myself.

Central Avenue had stores on both sides. From where we stood, I could see several pizza places. "Do we start here, or do we cross the street?" I asked Lexi.

She thought about it. "We might as well start here and then cross the street if we get desperate."

"That makes sense," I said. The first pizza place was only a few feet away.

"I'll go in with you," Lexi said. "But I think you'd better do the talking."

"Why?" I asked. I didn't want to be the one asking the questions.

"It'll give them a chance to hear your voice," Lexi explained.

I guessed that made sense. "Okay," I said. "But you have to come inside."

"I will," she said. "I won't leave you."

We went in. I never knew how scary a pizza parlor could be. It didn't matter that it was brightly lit and full of people. For that one minute, it was scary.

I walked over to the counter and stood absolutely still. I couldn't think what to say.

"Yeah?" the pizza man said.

It was almost as bad as when Mrs. Erdman had asked me what I was thinking about. My mouth opened, but no sound came out.

Lexi nudged me. I turned to her. "Ask if they deliver," she whispered.

I felt relieved. It was a safe question. "Do you deliver?" I asked.

"No," the guy said. "What do you want?"

"Nothing," I said. If we got a slice of pizza at every place on Central Avenue we'd end up looking like Mrs. Erdman. "Come on, Lexi. This isn't the right place."

Lexi followed me out. "You did that really well," she said.

"I couldn't have done it without you," I said. "I just froze."

"I would have frozen too," she said. "But the first one was bound to be the hardest. Next one you'll know how to start."

She was right. I wasn't quite as scared in the next place we went to. We walked right up to the counter and I asked, "Do you deliver?"

"Yes, we do," the guy said.

"Oh," I said. I wasn't prepared for that. "Uh, yesterday, did anybody call in a fake order? I mean around four-thirty."

"I wasn't in yesterday," the guy said. "Hey, Mario, were you here yesterday afternoon?"

"Yeah," a second man said. "Why?"

"Did anybody call in with a fake order?" the first man asked. "What kind of order?" he asked me.

"Six pizzas with everything on them," I said.

"Nah," Mario said. "I'd remember that if it happened."

"Thank you," I said.

"You see?" Lexi said. "It's getting easier and easier."

"I guess," I said. "But there are still a thousand pizza places left."

"Well, let's try the next one," Lexi said. "Maybe we'll be lucky."

We weren't. The third one didn't deliver and the fourth and fifth ones hadn't had any fake orders. I started to think about all the other pizza places, the ones by the supermarkets and at the malls and all the Italian restaurants that made pizza. I nearly started to cry.

"Six is my lucky number," Lexi said. "What's your lucky number?"

"I don't have a lucky number," I said. I wasn't feeling lucky about anything just then.

"What's your favorite number, then?" she asked. "I bet you have a favorite number."

"Eight," I said. "I like the number eight."

"Then it'll either be the sixth pizza place or the eighth," she said. "Or maybe the seventh because that's in between my six and your eight."

"Or maybe it'll be the sixty-eighth place," I

said. "Or the six hundredth place or the eight thousandth place."

"I don't think so," Lexi said. "I think it's going to be my lucky six or your favorite eight. Or maybe seven. Seven is supposed to be a lucky number too."

Six, seven, and eight all turned out to be unlucky, at least for us. Two of them didn't make deliveries and the third hadn't gotten a fake call the day before.

"Maybe we should quit now," Lexi said. "I really thought it would be six or eight."

"There's one more place left," I said. "Let's try that one. If it isn't the right place, I'll try calling from home."

"Okay," Lexi said. "But I don't know anyone whose lucky number is nine."

I walked into the pizza place, and Lexi followed me. This one was almost directly across the street from the first place we'd tried. If we'd crossed the street when we started it would have been the first place. That was the real reason I was so determined to go in.

I walked over to the counter and asked if they delivered.

"Yes, we do," the man said.

"Did anyone call in yesterday afternoon with a

fake order for a half dozen pizzas with everything on them?'' I asked.

The man stood absolutely still. ''You know something about that?'' he asked.

''Someone did?'' I said, trying not to sound excited.

''Harry!'' the man called. An older man walked over. ''Harry, this kid is asking about those pizzas.''

I told myself not to be scared, that I hadn't done it, that I was there to prove my innocence. But even so, I felt sick to my stomach.

''What do you know about that order?'' Harry asked.

''They think I did it,'' I said. ''And I didn't. I've been going to every pizza place on Central Avenue looking for the place that sent them. To prove I'm innocent.''

''I don't care if you're innocent or not,'' Harry said. ''That order was close to a hundred dollars. And I expect somebody to pay.''

''I'm sorry,'' I said, and I felt guilty all over again. ''I mean I didn't do it, but I'm really sorry.''

Lexi nudged me. ''Ask him about the order,'' she whispered. ''Ask him if he can identify your voice.''

She was right. That was why I was there, after all. "The order," I said. "Does my voice sound like the one that called?"

Harry turned to the younger man. "You took the order, Vinnie," he said. "What do you think?"

"How should I know?" Vinnie said. "It was a kid's voice over the phone. I wrote it down, got the address and the phone number, like I always do. I didn't pay no attention to the voice. I didn't expect to have to listen to no voice lineup."

"What did you do after you got the order?" I asked.

"I called right back," Vinnie said. "I don't send out no hundred-dollar order just because some kid calls. This is not the first kid who thinks it's a bright idea to call us up and put in a phony order."

"What happened when you called back?" I asked.

"Some dame answers and says yeah, she placed the order," Vinnie replied. "So I make the six pizzas and give them to Rocky, and he drives them over. Only they didn't place no six-pizzas-every-thing-on-them order. They won't pay for them. Lots of screaming. Rocky's got a mouth, the dame's got a mouth. They both call me. Not a damn thing I can do about it. Rocky comes back here, he's in a foul mood the rest of the night.

Harry's in a foul mood. I'm no singing angel myself. And we're stuck with six lousy pizzas and nobody to pay for them.''

"Did you keep the order?" I asked.

"You better believe it," Vinnie said. "Got it right here. Can I show it to her, Harry?"

"Sure, why not?" Harry said. "Let the kid see it."

Vinnie brought me the piece of paper he'd written the order on. I looked at it carefully. The word *Erdman* was written in capital letters. And the address was Elm Boulevard.

But the phone number was 555-9874. That wasn't right. Mrs. Erdman's number had a bunch of twos in it.

I felt like a fool. Of course whoever called hadn't used Mrs. Erdman's real number. There was too big a risk the pizza place would call back to confirm the order. I found a piece of paper and wrote down the number, then handed the original back to Vinnie.

Lexi nudged me again. "Ask Vinnie if he'll go to school and say you didn't do it," she whispered.

"Vinnie, would you go to my school and say I wasn't the one who called?" I asked.

Vinnie shook his head. "Like I said, it could've been you," he said. "I don't know. And I'm not about to go and say you're innocent and then find out you're guilty. We'll be out the hundred bucks because I said it wasn't you."

"Well, it wasn't," I said. "And I'm going to find out who it was and bring her back here. I promise."

"Do it," Vinnie said. "Bring that girl back here. 'Cause she owes us a hundred bucks and one big-time apology."

Chapter Seven

"**W**here have you been?" my mother said when I got home.

"Out," I said.

"*Out* is not an answer," my father said.

I knew I was in deep, deep trouble.

"I was with Lexi," I said. "We were just walking on Central Avenue. Walking and talking."

"I got a phone call today from Mrs. Delmonico," Mom said. "She told me all about the pizza order."

"Did she tell you I did it?" I asked. "Because if she did, she's lying. I didn't call in that order. I swear I didn't."

"Your principal is not a liar," Dad said. "What we need to find out is whether you are."

"Can we sit down?" I pleaded. It had been one of the worst days of my life, and it wasn't going to get any better with my parents grilling me.

Dad nodded. He, Mom, and I went into the living room. I caught the sound of a radio and realized Paul was hiding in his room. I wished I was with him.

"Did Mrs. Delmonico say I did it?" I asked, trying not to sound angry.

"She said someone called in a fake pizza order to your English teacher's house. She said the order was for close to a hundred dollars, and it was very upsetting to your teacher. . . . What is her name?" Dad said.

"Mrs. Erdman," Mom said.

"Mrs. Erdman," Dad repeated. "Her husband is recuperating from surgery and she's quite upset. And while you denied ordering the pizza, you admitted that you were angry at Mrs. Erdman for punishing you yesterday, and that ordering the pizza was your idea. Mrs. Delmonico also said that although she didn't know it for a fact, she suspected you were responsible."

"I'm not!" I shouted. "The reason she didn't know it for a fact is because it isn't true."

"She said the pizzas were ordered yesterday around four-thirty," Mom said. "I know you weren't home then because I called from the office to say I'd be a few minutes late and Paul said you weren't here. So where were you?"

I hesitated for a moment. I hated the thought of lying to my parents, especially when I'd just called Mrs. Delmonico a liar. I wanted so much for them to believe me when I said I was innocent.

On the other hand, I wasn't about to tell them I'd been hiding in a stairwell waiting to find Dad's girlfriend so that I could send her the pizzas. What had been easy for me to tell Lexi was the hardest thing in the world for me to say to my parents.

"I told you yesterday," I said. "I was at the library. With Lexi."

"Who's this Lexi you keep talking about?" Mom asked. "I don't know anybody named Lexi."

"Lexi Richards," I said. There was no point in claiming that Mom should remember her name. "She's kind of new. We ran into each other at the library yesterday and we got to talking. This afternoon we decided to spend some more time together."

"Walking on Central Avenue," Mom said. "I

don't remember your ever walking on Central Avenue just for the fun of it.''

"It was Lexi's idea," I said.

"I don't remember your ever just going to the library," Dad said. "Why did you?"

"I went to see about a book," I said, which was true, even if the book was a phone book. "Isn't that why people go to libraries, to see about books?"

"Did you take the book out?" Mom asked.

"No," I admitted.

"So we have no way of knowing whether you really were at the library," Mom said.

"I met Branwell's mother," I said. "She's a librarian there and her dog is named Branwell. She said I should say hi to Dad for her but I forgot."

"Branwell," Dad said. "That's Meg Daley's dog. She does work at the library. I'm going to call there now and ask to speak to her."

"No, don't do that, Dad," I said.

"And why not?" he asked.

"Because it would be embarrassing," I said.

"That's not a reason," he said. "Not at this point." He walked into the kitchen to find the phone book and look up the library's number. Once he did that, I could hear him ask for Margaret Daley. He asked if I'd been at the library yesterday, and then he thanked her and hung up.

"Taryn was at the library, all right," Dad said. "Meg Daley works at the reference desk. Taryn went there and asked to use the phone book. She looked up several numbers and wrote them down. Mrs. Daley isn't sure what Taryn did next, but she thought she remembered Taryn leaving the library right away."

"But she isn't sure," I said. "That's because I saw Lexi and went over to her."

"What were you looking up in the phone book?" Mom asked. "Whose number was so important to you?"

For a second I thought it would serve them right if I told them the truth. Then the whispers would turn to shouts.

But that scared me, made me as frightened as I'd ever been of anything. "I just looked up some people's numbers," I said. "It was nothing important."

"It was important enough for you to go to the library," Dad said.

"Did you look up Mrs. Erdman's number?" Mom asked. "Were you looking for her address to order those pizzas?"

"No," I said. "I didn't order the pizzas." It was the one true thing I could say.

"Then whose number were you looking up?" Dad asked.

"I don't remember," I said. "It wasn't that important."

I couldn't remember ever seeing Dad so angry. I kept telling myself that I was innocent, that I hadn't ordered the pizzas, but it didn't help. Sometimes the truth doesn't count as much if it's surrounded by lies.

"Let me ask something else," Mom said, sounding almost reasonable compared to Dad. "What did you do that made Mrs. Erdman punish you yesterday?"

"I didn't do anything," I said. "She's mean. She's a terrible teacher. She likes to humiliate kids for no reason. She's done it to Lexi too. We both hate her."

"Is that why you and Lexi are such good friends?" Mom asked. "Because you both dislike Mrs. Erdman?"

"I don't know," I said. "I just like her. She's fun."

"This isn't about Lexi," Dad said. "It's about you and Mrs. Erdman. Are you saying you did absolutely nothing wrong and Mrs. Erdman simply decided to punish you for the pure joy of it?''

''I was thinking about something,'' I said. ''And I was looking out the window and not paying attention and Mrs. Erdman got mad. That's all. That's my big crime. I wasn't paying attention. I'm sorry. Do I get the electric chair or lethal injection?''

''Sarcasm isn't going to help you,'' Dad said. ''I suggest you cut it out right now.''

''I'm sorry,'' I said. ''But really that's all that happened. I was looking out the window, and Mrs. Erdman went crazy.''

''And how did she punish you?'' Mom asked.

''She told me to tell the class what I was thinking about, and I wouldn't. It wasn't anything important and it wasn't anybody's business. So she made me stand in front of the class until I told. The kids made fun of me and she didn't stop them. I cried and she still wouldn't let me sit down. When class ended she told me I had to write a thousand-word composition on what I'd been thinking about and hand it in to her this morning.''

''I'd like to read that composition,'' Dad said. ''I assume since Mrs. Erdman wasn't in school today you still have it.''

''I never wrote it,'' I said.

"Why not?" he asked. "You were specifically told to. Was that part of getting back at her, not following her instructions?"

"No," I said. "I meant to write it. I just forgot."

"You forgot?" he asked. "You were so upset you were driven to tears, and then you forgot?"

"I'll write it tonight," I said. "I promise. And I'll give it to her tomorrow morning. She won't know I didn't write it when I was supposed to."

"Let me see if I have this straight," Dad said. "In English yesterday you were daydreaming and Mrs. Erdman called on you. When she realized you weren't paying attention she demanded to know what you were thinking about. You wouldn't tell her, even though it wasn't anything important. Mrs. Erdman made you stand in front of the class until you told. Everyone made fun of you and Mrs. Erdman presumably let them."

"It wasn't everybody," I said. "It was Billy Fleming. But all the kids laughed at what he said. So it felt like it was everybody."

"All right," Dad said. "Billy Fleming made fun of you. You cried and Mrs. Erdman didn't excuse you. You had to keep standing there. Then the class ended and Mrs. Erdman gave you the assignment of writing a thousand words on what you were thinking about.''

I nodded.

''Then you had lunch and during lunch you came up with this pizza idea,'' Dad said. ''Because you were so mad at Mrs. Erdman. Who did you talk about it with?''

''Heather and Nicole,'' I said. ''But they didn't do it either. They were at their Girl Scout meeting.''

''After school you went to the library to look up somebody in the phone book,'' Dad said. ''Only you no longer remember who. You met Lexi there, the two of you talked, and you came home in such a good mood that you forgot all about the thousand-word composition. Is that it?''

I nodded.

''You weren't in a good mood last night,'' Mom said. ''You hardly spoke at supper. I asked you if you had any homework and you said you'd done it all already, and that was the only thing you said. I remember being a little worried about you, you were so quiet.''

''You certainly didn't say anything about Mrs. Erdman, or meeting Lexi at the library,'' Dad said. ''And if you and Lexi were at the library talking the whole time, when did you do your home-work?''

"I didn't order the pizzas!'' I cried. "Why won't you just believe me?''

"We want to believe you,'' Mom said. "But you're not making it easy for us.''

"I think we should call this Lexi person,'' Dad said. "She can tell us if what Taryn's saying is true.''

"Don't do that, Dad,'' I said.

"And why not?'' he asked.

I didn't really have an answer. Lexi would prob-ably back me up in all my lies. But maybe she'd tell Dad what I'd been thinking about in school the day before. Maybe she'd tell about Lisa Brown and my attempt at spying.

"I don't know her phone number,'' I said. "Look, you're right about something. We didn't just walk up and down on Central Avenue this af-ternoon. We went to all the pizza places there to see if we could find the one that sent the pizza to Mrs. Erdman.''

"And did you?'' Dad asked.

"We sure did,'' I said. "Only the guy couldn't say for sure it wasn't me who made the call. But would we have tried finding the place if I had done it?''

78

"You spoke to the person who took the order, only he couldn't be sure whether it was your voice or not. That's what you're telling us?" Dad asked.

I nodded. "He told us all about the call. And how Rocky went over with the delivery and everybody got mad at everybody. I could see he thought I was innocent."

"Rocky thought you were innocent?" Dad said.

"No, Vinnie did," I said. "I think Harry did too. I didn't meet Rocky."

"Maybe we should meet Vinnie," Mom said. "And Harry. And Rocky."

"No, that's not such a good idea," Dad said. "They might think if we went over there it was because we intended to pay them for the pizzas. Which we don't. Even if Taryn did do it. She'll pay for them herself, without any help from us."

"I don't have a hundred dollars!" I said.

"Then you'll earn it," Dad said. "You have to learn to be responsible for your actions and not count on us to bail you out."

The last thing I'd been doing was counting on my parents. I almost told them that too. Instead I said, "Look, I didn't do it. I was mad at Mrs. Erdman, I admit that. But I didn't order those pizzas. I tried to find out who did. Lexi and I figured the first step was to find the girl who made the call, and the best way of doing that was by finding the pizza place. We found the pizza place. They even gave us the phone number of the person who put in the call.''

"They did?'' Dad said. "You have that number?''

"Yes,'' I said, and I dug it out of my pocket. "Here it is. 555-9874.''

"Maybe that's Mrs. Erdman's number,'' Mom said. "Maybe there's just been some big mix-up.''

"No, it isn't,'' Dad said. "I looked up *Erdman* in the phone book before I called the library. To see if Taryn could have found it. Which she could have. This number is different.''

"Then let's call the number and see who answers,'' Mom said. "If it's some other girl in Taryn's class, then we'll know for sure that Taryn is innocent.''

"That's what I was going to do,'' I said. "That's why I got the number from Vinnie.''

We all went to the kitchen phone. Mom punched in the number. We could hear the phone ring half a dozen times, but nobody picked up.

"That's odd,'' Mom said. "It's so close to dinnertime, you'd think people would be home.''

"It might be a pay phone,'' Dad said. "The girl might have called from a pay phone and then stuck around to answer it when the pizza place called back.''

"Does that mean you believe me?" I asked. "That I wasn't the one who did it?"

Dad sighed. "I'd certainly like to believe that," he said. "But you have to admit, Taryn, there's a lot in your story that doesn't make sense."

Paul came out of his room then, which was a relief. I didn't know how I was going to separate the parts of the story that were true from the lies.

"What's going on?" he asked, nice and casual.

"Someone sent a half dozen pizzas to Mrs. Erdman's—Taryn's English teacher's—house," Mom said. "The principal thinks it might have been Taryn, but she says she didn't do it."

"Mrs. Erdman *is* pretty mean. Boring too," Paul said.

"She's even worse now than when you had her," I said.

"Did you order those pizzas?" Paul asked me.

"No," I said.

"Okay," he said. "Just as long as you didn't, it'll work out."

"I hope so," Dad said. "For everybody's sake, I hope you're right."

Chapter Eight

That evening, while Mom and Dad took turns standing over me, I wrote a thousand words on what I'd been thinking about when I should have been paying attention.

I wrote about my birthday and what kind of party I wanted and the presents I was hoping I'd get. My birthday was almost six weeks away, and I hadn't really thought about it at all, but it was the safest thing I could think of to write about.

When I finished the composition, Dad and Mom both read it.

"Do you really want your own TV and VCR?" Mom asked when she was through reading.

"No," I said, although of course I did. I just didn't think I had a chance of getting it.

"Good," she said. "Because you don't have a chance of getting it."

What I really wanted was a one-way ticket out of there, but I had even less chance of getting that. Instead I had two hovering parents. At least they weren't whispering.

After I'd gone to bed that night, Mom came into my room.

"Your father and I don't know what to do," she said. "We're pretty sure you're lying about some things, but we don't know which things and we don't know what exactly you have done and what you haven't, so we don't know what punishment is appropriate."

I couldn't blame her. By that point, I wasn't sure myself what I'd done and what I hadn't. "I didn't order the pizzas," I said. That was the one thing I knew.

"We want to believe you," Mom said. "But since there are so many things you're not being open about, we just don't know. You did come up with the idea, Taryn. And there's obviously something bothering you. Do you want to talk to me about it?"

If I'd wanted to talk to her about it, I would have done it already. "Nothing's bothering me," I said. "Except that people think I did something when I didn't."

Mom looked down at me. None of this was her fault, I knew, and I felt terrible that I was making her feel worse. "Is any of this about—" she began, but then she stopped herself. "No, it couldn't be," she said instead.

I didn't ask her to finish her thought. I could have, and then maybe we would have talked honestly and the whispering would have ended. But I couldn't. As long as she and Dad didn't talk to me about it, I could tell myself none of it was real. I was so scared Mom would say she and Dad were getting a divorce that I said, "I didn't order those pizzas," just to change the subject.

"I'm not saying that you did," Mom replied. "But if you did, I want you to know your father and I will still love you. We'll be angry, because whoever ordered those pizzas played a cruel practical joke, and we don't approve of that sort of behavior. If we find out it was you, you'll be responsible for the cost, and you'll have to apologize, and we'll find an appropriate punishment. But we'd be doing it because we love you, not because we're vindictive. And I like to think you know that ordering the pizzas was the wrong thing to do."

"It was the wrong thing to do," I said. "I know that. That's why I didn't do it."

"I hope you're telling the truth," Mom said. "I just wish you'd tell us the truth about everything."

"I'm tired," I said. "Can I go to sleep now?"

Mom bent over and gave me a kiss. "Sleep well," she said. "See you in the morning."

At breakfast Mom and Dad hardly said a word to each other. And if they weren't talking, there didn't seem to be much reason for Paul or me to say anything.

I left for school early. I had to hand in my composition to Mrs. Erdman, and I didn't much feel like talking to anybody on the way. I was relieved when I didn't see Heather, Nicole, or Lexi on my way in. I just wasn't ready to talk to any of them.

I went right to Mrs. Erdman's room. She was sitting at her desk staring out the window. Seeing her like that made me want to laugh. She looked the way I had two days earlier, but no one was punishing her for daydreaming.

I walked into the room, but she didn't seem to notice me. I said, "Excuse me."

Mrs. Erdman turned around. "What do you want?" she asked.

"I have that composition you asked for."

"What composition?" she asked.

"The one on what I was thinking about," I said. "A thousand words on what I was thinking about."

"Oh, that's right," she said. "I'd forgotten."

"Here it is," I said, handing it to her.

She took it from me and glanced at it. "You were thinking about your birthday?" she asked. She didn't sound nearly as mean as usual. If she had, I would have kept on lying.

"No," I admitted. "I wasn't."

"But you wrote about that anyway," she said. "That's what it says here, that your birthday was on your mind."

"I had to put something down," I said. "And my parents were watching me, so I didn't want to write about what I was really thinking about."

"All right," she said. "At this point it doesn't really matter. Thoughts should be private. No one should be able to steal them from you."

I stared at her. Mrs. Erdman had been absent the day before. Maybe creatures from outer space had stolen her body and put in one of their own souls. That might not be good for Mrs. Erdman, but it would make my school year a whole lot easier.

"I'm sorry about the pizzas," I said to Pod Person Erdman. "I didn't order them, but I'm sorry it happened."

Mrs. Erdman stared at me. Then she burst into tears.

I was totally unprepared for that. It had never occurred to me that Mrs. Erdman even knew how to cry. I'd never seen a teacher cry before.

"Don't cry," I said. "They'll find out who ordered those pizzas. I'm trying to find out myself."

She didn't stop crying. I started to panic. The school bell would be ringing in a minute or two, and Mrs. Erdman was crying the way Lexi and I had been laughing the day before. She was crying nonstop, totally crazy tears.

I looked around for a box of tissues, but she didn't have one. It wouldn't have helped anyway, I figured. There was nothing I could do to help, so I decided to leave.

I'd made it to the door when Mrs. Delmonico came in. There I was, looking as if I'd committed every unsolved crime in America, and there was Mrs. Erdman sobbing her head off.

"Mrs. Erdman, are you all right?" Mrs. Delmonico asked.

Mrs. Erdman didn't answer.

"I'm going to get the nurse," Mrs. Delmonico said. "Stay where you are. Taryn, come with me, right now!"

"Yes, Mrs. Delmonico," I said. I followed her to her office and watched as she called the nurse. I hoped the nurse carried tissues with her.

"I think I've put up with enough from you, Taryn," Mrs. Delmonico said after she hung up the phone. "It's bad enough your playing a nasty practical joke like that. But to make Mrs. Erdman cry? I don't even want to know what you said to her. It doesn't matter. I'm calling your parents right now and suspending you for the day."

"What?" I said.

"And don't give me any backtalk, or that suspension will last a lot longer," Mrs. Delmonico said. "Just because I didn't punish you yesterday doesn't mean you got away with something."

"I didn't order the pizzas," I said.

"And you didn't make Mrs. Erdman cry either, I suppose," Mrs. Delmonico said. "What did you do, run into her room, say something cruel, and then think you could just get away?"

"I didn't do anything wrong!" I shouted.

"Then you have a very strange sense of right and wrong," she said. "Give me your mother's phone number."

I did. Mrs. Delmonico called, but Mom hadn't gotten to work yet.

"I'll try your father," she said. "Give me his number."

It made me sick, but I did. I hated to think that Lisa would answer the call and tell Dad my principal wanted to talk to him.

"Taryn is under a one-day suspension," Mrs. Delmonico told Dad. "I've been unable to reach your wife, so I need you to come to school and get her."

Mrs. Delmonico left the office for a few minutes, then came back. "Mrs. Erdman went home," she said. "She didn't feel up to teaching today."

"Did she tell you it wasn't my fault?" I asked.

"She was still crying," Mrs. Delmonico said. "We had to call a doctor, she was so upset."

"But I didn't do it," I said. "I didn't do anything."

"That's getting to be a tired song," Mrs. Delmonico said. "The sooner you confess, the better off you'll be, Taryn."

For a minute I thought about confessing. She was probably right. I knew most of what would happen to me if I said I'd sent the pizzas. Mom had said there'd be an additional punishment. I'd probably be grounded for a month or something like that. Maybe no birthday party. Maybe instead of presents they'd help pay for the pizzas. I could live with that.

Then I realized I'd have to apologize to everybody. To Mrs. Erdman, to my parents, and to Mrs. Delmonico. Even that would be okay, since I'd know it was a lie, but that was all any of them deserved.

But I didn't want to have to apologize to Vinnie and Harry. They were the only ones who might be willing to believe that I hadn't done it. And it drove me crazy thinking about going to their pizza parlor with my parents to tell them I made the order and I was sorry and would pay them back.

It would have been bad enough if I'd done it, but to do it when I was innocent, to even think about doing it, drove me crazy.

By the time Dad got to Mrs. Delmonico's office, I was ready to kill. I sat there quietly while my brain raced at a million miles an hour. I was innocent. Sure I'd lied, but every lie I'd told was because I was innocent. No one should have to lie when they're innocent. It was everyone else who was making me lie, and now they were going to punish me even more.

If telling the truth got you in trouble, I was going

to keep on lying until the day I died. Why not? Everyone else lied. Dad was lying to Mom, and Mom was lying to me, and Mrs. Erdman was lying when she kept crying instead of saying I hadn't done anything. They were all liars, liars, liars, no better than me. Probably worse, because I was innocent and they were all guilty. Well, maybe Mom wasn't, but Dad sure was, and so was Mrs. Erdman, and I hated all of them.

Dad stormed into Mrs. Delmonico's office. "What's she done this time?" he asked.

"She said something cruel to Mrs. Erdman," Mrs. Delmonico said. "I don't know what because poor Mrs. Erdman was so hysterical she couldn't speak."

"Taryn?" Dad said.

I didn't say a word. Talking wasn't going to do me any good.

"Taryn's suspension will be put in her permanent records," Mrs. Delmonico said. "I need you to sign this paper, right here. Thank you, Dr. Powell."

"Taryn will be in school tomorrow with a full apology to Mrs. Erdman," Dad said. "Written and verbal. I promise you that, Mrs. Delmonico. And if we find out she was responsible for the pizzas, we'll inform you immediately."

"Thank you," Mrs. Delmonico said. "I'll be in touch with you shortly."

Dad nodded and told me to get up. I followed him out of the school building to his car.

"We're going to have a long talk," he said, "and straighten things out once and for all. Do you hear me, Taryn?"

I got into the car and slammed the door.

"Very well," Dad said. "We'll have this conversation at home. But don't think you can avoid giving me some honest answers. Because I'm sick of this whole situation, and I'm going to get to the bottom of it before the day is done."

Just try, I thought. Just you try.

Chapter Nine

Neither one of us opened our mouths during the drive home. When we got there, Dad called Mom from the kitchen.

"Your mother is at a meeting," he said to me after he'd hung up. "I told them to have her call me when she's through."

"Are you going back to the office now?" I asked. This suspension might not be so bad if I was left alone.

"I'll stay here at least until your mother gets home," he said. "This isn't a holiday, Taryn. This is very serious, and it's going to get more so unless we get to the bottom of your actions."

I'd thought I had already gotten to the bottom.

What could be worse than being suspended for making a teacher cry when you didn't and being told over and over again that you'd done something wrong when you hadn't?

Dad and I sat down in the living room. I looked at him carefully and thought about how much I used to love him. I wondered if I ever would again.

He closed his eyes, which I knew meant he was thinking about what he wanted to say. I wanted him to shout. I wanted to scream right back at him.

But he didn't shout. "I thought I knew you pretty well," he said. "I thought you were a good girl. I thought you were someone who knew the difference between right and wrong."

I'd thought the same about him. But now I had my doubts. I kept quiet.

"Did you deliberately make Mrs. Erdman cry?" he asked. "Did you say something cruel to get back at her in some way?"

"No," I said.

"What did you say to her, then? Mrs. Delmonico was extremely upset, and I gather Mrs. Erdman is in a very bad way. What did you say that made her cry?"

"I didn't say anything," I said. "I gave her my stupid composition."

"And she burst into tears?" Dad asked.

"Just about," I said.

"So there was some conversation," Dad said. "Why don't you just tell me what the two of you said, and then we can figure out why Mrs. Erdman began crying."

"I don't know why she cried," I said. "Maybe it's because she's crazy. But it wasn't anything I said."

"Indulge me," Dad said. "Tell me what the two of you talked about."

"We talked about my composition," I said. "I gave it to her and I said, 'Here it is,' or something like that, and she didn't even seem to remember it. I had to tell her why I'd written it. It took me hours to write that thing and she didn't even remember."

"Did you get mad at her for that?" Dad asked.

"Of course I did," I said. "I'm always mad at Mrs. Erdman. I hate her."

"Did you say that to her?" he asked. He didn't sound angry anymore, just puzzled. I thought about how puzzled I'd been when Mrs. Erdman hadn't been mean to me, and I realized Dad probably thought the pod people had taken over my body as well.

"I didn't make her cry," I said. "We actually talked for a minute about the composition and then I told her I hadn't ordered the pizzas and that's when she started crying. I didn't know what to do, so I figured I might as well just leave. I was almost out of the room when Mrs. Delmonico walked in. All she saw was me and Mrs. Erdman crying, so she figured I was to blame. Only I wasn't. Mrs. Erdman was behaving kind of weird when I first walked in. I think she's sick. But I didn't make her sick and I didn't make her cry and I didn't order those pizzas.''

"It always comes back to those pizzas,'' Dad said. "And how you keep denying having anything to do with them.''

"I keep denying it because it's true,'' I said. "I didn't order them, no matter what you think.''

"I don't know what to think anymore,'' Dad said. "All I know is someone played a cruel practical joke on Mrs. Erdman and it was your idea. That at least you admit.''

"But I didn't do it! There's a difference between saying you want to do something and actually doing it.''

"Yes, there is,'' Dad said. "But it's obvious to me and just about everybody else that you're lying about certain things. You say you went to the library to see about a book, but it turns out the book was the phone book and you claim you don't remember whose number you were looking up.

That's obviously a lie. And there are other things that don't make sense about what you did Monday afternoon. You say you were with this girl Lexi and the two of you had a great time, but when you came home you didn't mention Lexi and you were in a bad mood and your homework was all done.''

"I wasn't in a bad mood," I said. "I was just quiet. And I did my homework before I went to the library."

"And you forgot all about the composition," Dad said. "You're doing a lot of selective forgetting, Taryn. Maybe you just forgot about ordering those pizzas."

"I never ordered those pizzas!" I shouted. "Why won't you believe me? You're my father. You're supposed to believe me. Lexi believed me and she hardly even knows me."

Dad stared at me. "I thought Lexi knew you couldn't have ordered them because the two of you were together," he said.

"That's what I meant," I said, but I knew it was too late.

"You weren't with Lexi at the library," Dad said. "I know that doesn't mean you ordered the pizzas, but, Taryn, I have to know where you were. Whose number were you looking up in the phone book?"

"Lisa's," I said.

"Lisa?" Dad said. "Lisa who?"

"Lisa Brown," I said. "Your receptionist, Lisa."

"Why were you looking her number up?" Dad asked. "Why didn't you just call her at the office?"

"I didn't want her number," I said. "I wanted her address. I wanted to see where she lived. But there were four different listings in the phone book and I didn't know which one was her so I picked one of them and waited at her apartment for her to show up. I hid in the stairwell, and I did my homework there, only I forgot about the composition. And I picked the wrong L. Brown. It wasn't Lisa's apartment, so I came home."

"I still don't understand why you were waiting around for Lisa," Dad said. "If you wanted to know where she lived, you could have called her at the office to get her address."

"I was going to send her the pizzas," I said. "But I didn't want the wrong L. Brown to get them."

"But why would you want to play a practical joke on Lisa?" Dad asked. "What's she ever done to you?"

"I know what's going on, Dad," I said. "I can hear you and Mom whispering at night."

Dad's jaw dropped. I'd never seen him look so shocked.

"Paul and I talked about it," I said, trying not to cry. "He said you and Lisa are having an affair. I was afraid you were going to leave us. I thought maybe if I was mean to Lisa, she'd leave town and you wouldn't see her anymore."

"My God," Dad said.

"Lexi lied for me," I said. "She saw me at the library and she said I stayed there with her when I didn't. But I never ordered those pizzas and I don't know who did."

"Paul thinks Lisa and I are having an affair?" Dad asked. "He actually said that to you?"

"Sunday night," I said. "That's what I was thinking about when Mrs. Erdman called on me. I was thinking about you and Lisa and what it would be like if you divorced Mom. But I couldn't tell her that. I couldn't stand in front of the whole class and tell them all that. Heather and Nicole don't even know."

"Stop," Dad said. "Just stop for a moment, all right? I really need a moment right now."

I went into the kitchen and poured myself a glass

of milk. I drank it, rinsed out the glass, and went back to the living room.

"Lisa and I are not having an affair," Dad said after I sat down again. "That's the first thing I want to say. I am not cheating on your mother, nor would I ever. I happen to take my marriage vows very seriously, as does your mother."

"But the two of you are fighting," I said. "And you're fighting about Lisa."

Dad took a deep breath. "That's true," he said. "And I wish it wasn't. And it isn't because your mother is crazy or because she just misunderstood something. I've had some feelings about Lisa and your mother knows that and she's very upset about it. And we've been fighting about that, and about other things as well, things that have nothing to do with Lisa. Your mother wants me to sell this practice and open up a bigger one with the vet near your grandparents. I think that would be a mistake. This is not a good time in our marriage, and we didn't want you kids to know, so we tried to keep our fighting to ourselves. I can see we've done a very bad job of it."

"Are you going to get a divorce?" I asked.

Dad shook his head. "I love your mother," he said. "And she loves me and we're both committed to this marriage. She's been talking about counseling and I've been fighting the idea, but now I can see it might be the right thing. We didn't want you kids to know. We didn't want you to suffer because of our problems. And we failed, and that hurts a lot.''

"It hurts me too,'' I said. "Daddy, I've been so scared.''

"I'm so sorry,'' he said, reaching out to hug me. "I'm more sorry than you can know. I love you so much, Taryn.''

It felt so wonderful to be hugged by my father and to know he wanted to work things out, that he really did love Mom and Paul and me. And it felt unbelievably great to tell the truth after all those lies I'd thought I'd have to tell forever.

Just as I was starting to feel really okay, the phone rang. We both jumped, and then we laughed.

"That's probably your mother,'' Dad said, and went to the kitchen to answer. But I guessed from his end of the conversation that it wasn't.

"It was Mrs. Delmonico,'' he said when he got off the phone. "She called to say Mrs. Erdman called from the doctor's office. Mrs. Erdman said she wouldn't be back to school today. She needed another day off to recover from all the stress in her life.''

That was pretty much how I felt. It almost made

me laugh to think that Mrs. Erdman and I might have something in common.

"Mrs. Delmonico said she asked Mrs. Erdman what you'd done to make her cry, and Mrs. Erdman said you hadn't done anything at all. She said she was hardly even aware you were in the room. It had nothing to do with you at all."

"She really said that?" I asked. I knew it was the truth, but it was hard to imagine Mrs. Erdman ever doing anything that might help me.

"That's what she said," Dad replied. "Mrs. Delmonico said she'd erase the suspension from your record, since she was wrong about the whole incident. She wanted to know if you would come back to school today."

"Do I have to?" I asked.

Dad thought about it, but before he got around to answering, the phone rang again. This time it was Mom.

Dad talked with her for a few minutes. "Your mother is going to take the rest of the day off from work," he said. "And I'm going to stay here until lunchtime so that the three of us can talk. We have a lot that needs to be talked about. Including all those lies you told and what we're going to do about them."

I nodded.

"We're going to talk," Dad said. "Not shout, not scream, and certainly not whisper. There's going to be no more whispering in this household. The whispering days are over."

Chapter Ten

My family went out for supper that night.

"I'm not sure what we're celebrating," Dad said. "But I think it's something important."

I knew what I felt good about. Even though my parents thought that I should be punished for all my lies, they finally believed I hadn't ordered the pizzas. They agreed to be more open about their problems, and they assured me they had every intention of staying married. When Paul had come home from school, they'd told him exactly the same things.

"It would be nice if we knew who really ordered those pizzas," Mom said at supper. "I think that's the only way you can really clear your name, Taryn.''

''And you are going to have to tell Mrs. Delmonico you lied about your alibi,'' Dad said. ''There's been too much lying going on. You're going to have to accept the consequences.''

''But that'll get Lexi in trouble too,'' I said. ''She lied first.''

''Do you think Lexi ordered the pizzas?'' Paul asked.

''I've been wondering about that also,'' Mom said.

''She couldn't have,'' I said. ''I mean, why would she?''

''When she gave you an alibi, she gave herself one too,'' Mom said. ''That's what's been bothering me.''

''And you did say Mrs. Erdman picked on her too,'' Dad said. ''I wish we knew more about Lexi.''

''She's really nice,'' I said. ''And she helped me find the pizza place. She lied for me because she likes me.''

But when I thought about it, I saw their point. Lexi had refused to talk in any of the pizza places. She had suggested we start on the wrong side of the street. And she'd thought we should quit after the eighth pizza parlor, when it turned out the ninth one was the right one.

Mom was right about the alibi. As long as Lexi said the two of us were together, it meant she couldn't have called in the order.

But I didn't want it to be Lexi any more than I'd wanted it to be Heather or Nicole. Lexi hadn't been my friend for very long, but I wanted our friendship to grow. She understood me and made me laugh and I could tell her things I couldn't even tell Heather or Nicole.

"It isn't Lexi," I said. "I just know it."

"I don't suppose you happen to know who it is, then?" Dad said.

I shook my head. "It's just not Lexi. She wouldn't do something mean. She isn't a mean person."

"Neither are you," Paul said. "But everybody was sure willing to believe you did it."

"I know," I said.

Paul laughed. "I'm sorry. It's just the image of Mrs. Erdman sobbing hysterically and Taryn trying to escape and running into Mrs. Delmonico."

"I wasn't running," I said, but when Dad and Mom laughed, I did too.

"Mom, I thought big girls didn't cry," Paul said.

"Mrs. Erdman isn't a girl," Mom said, and laughed even harder.

"I don't get it," I said. "What about big girls?"

"You know, that song they play sometimes," Paul said. "On the oldies station. 'Big Girls Don't Cry.' " He sang all funny and weird.

Mom laughed even harder. "You're no Frankie Valli," she said.

"Who's Frankie Valli?" I asked.

"He was the lead singer for the Four Seasons," Mom said. " 'Big Girls Don't Cry' was one of their big hits."

"He had quite a falsetto," Dad said. "Those *yiy yiy yiy*s of his could break glass."

"What's a falsetto?" I asked. It was annoying not to get the joke.

"It's when a man sings in a really high-pitched voice," Dad said.

"Yiy yiy yiy," Paul sang, which only made Mom laugh harder.

"Men can sing like women?" I asked.

"Some men can," Dad said. "There's one guy I've seen on TV who does great impressions of Barbra Streisand and Judy Garland. And a lot of the old rock stars sang falsetto sometimes."

Suddenly I knew who'd ordered the pizzas. "Can we go home now?" I said. "I have to make like a zillion phone calls."

"Not before dessert," Dad and Paul said in unison, which made us all laugh.

"Who do you have to call?" Mom asked. "Frankie Valli?"

"The pizza place," I said. "I'm almost a hundred percent sure who ordered those pizzas. But I have to talk to Vinnie."

"That's nearly enough to make me cancel dessert," Dad said. Just then the waiter brought ice cream for Paul and me and a hunk of strawberry cheesecake for Mom and Dad to share. "Good thing I said *nearly*."

We wolfed our desserts and drove home.

I called the pizza place and asked to talk to Vinnie. When he came to the phone, I reminded him who I was.

"You figure out who made the order?" he asked.

"I think so," I said. "Are you sure it was a girl?"

I could picture him thinking about it. "The kid had a high-pitched voice," he replied. "I figured it had to be a girl."

"How about a falsetto?" I asked. "Someone like Frankie Valli?"

"You mean the Four Seasons guy?" Vinnie asked. *"Yiy yiy yiy?"*

"That's the one," I said.

"Could be," Vinnie said. "I wasn't paying that much attention. I knew it was a kid, and I knew I was going to have to call back, so I was just writing down what she, or maybe he, was saying."

"And the voice when you called back?" I asked.

"Now that you mention it, it was kind of strange," Vinnie said. "I was sure it wasn't the same kid, or else I wouldn't have made the pizzas. But the voice sounded kind of phony. Grown-up, but sort of stuck-up. I just figured it was some rich snob. I wasn't thinking it was some joke."

"Do you think it could have been a boy both times?" I asked. "Don't say yes unless you really think it could."

"A boy," Vinnie said. "Like Frankie Valli. Yeah, it could've been. I'm not saying it was, but it could've been."

"Thank you," I said. "If I'm right, I'll know tomorrow who did it."

"Well, send him over here when you do," Vinnie said. "We're still out that hundred bucks and none of us is getting any happier about it."

I thanked him, got off the phone, and told my family what Vinnie had said.

"What if you're right?" Paul asked. "Are you going to tell Mrs. Delmonico on him?"

"I can't prove anything," I said. "He might just deny it."

"But what if you did know?" Mom asked. "Would you tell then?"

I thought about how angry I'd been when Heather and Nicole had admitted hearing me come up with the pizza plan. "No," I said. "I'm not going to tell."

"Your name won't be cleared until you can prove who really did it," Dad said. "Are you ready to live with the consequences of that?"

I wasn't. The thought of seeing Mrs. Erdman scared me. And as long as Mrs. Delmonico thought I'd ordered the pizzas, I knew I'd be blamed for all kinds of things I'd had nothing to do with. I didn't want to spend the rest of my life under threat of suspension. And running away didn't seem like such a good idea either.

"Maybe I could trick him," I said. "Maybe I could get him to confess in front of lots of people."

"Maybe you could," Mom said. "Let's see if we can figure out how."

By the time I went to bed, the plan was set.

110

Everyone knew what they were supposed to do. I could only hope it all worked out.

The next day I saw Heather and Nicole in the schoolyard. They were standing together, giggling. I walked right over to them.

"Talking about me?" I said angrily.

"Why would we do that?" Heather asked, then glanced at Nicole.

"I figured you're trying to decide what else to say about me," I said. "I know you told Mrs. Delmonico the pizzas were my idea."

"Well, they were," Nicole said.

"You still didn't have to tell! I got suspended thanks to you."

"Don't blame us," Heather said. "You're the one who started all this."

"All I know is real friends wouldn't have told on me!" I shouted.

"If you were my real friend, you wouldn't be blaming me for something you did!" Nicole shouted back.

"Taryn's like that," Heather said. "She's always whining, 'It's not my fault, it's not my fault.' It doesn't matter what the truth is, she's never to blame."

"If that's what you really think about me, I don't want to be your friend anymore," I said.

"Good," Heather said. "Because I haven't wanted to be friends with you for a long time."

"Me neither," Nicole said. "Come on, Heather. We have better things to do."

"Heather, Nicole," I called, but they just walked away.

I felt as if the whole school had seen us fighting. It was all anybody talked about that morning. Even Lexi kept away from me. I'd never felt so alone in my life.

It was almost impossible for me to pay attention during my first three classes. I wondered what everybody thought about me. Did they all assume I'd ordered the pizzas, and that I was such a big liar that even my friends wouldn't stick by me? So much depended on the plan.

The second I got to English class, I saw my parents waiting. Now I knew everyone would be talking about me.

"I'm Taryn's father," Dad said. "My wife and I want to see Mrs. Delmonico, and we want Taryn to be with us."

"What?" Mrs. Erdman said. "Yes, there's plenty to talk about. Taryn, you may go with your parents."

I was terrified. Mom held my hand as we walked down the corridor to see Mrs. Delmonico. "Just

112

think how good it will feel when your name is cleared,'' Mom said.

I tried to take her advice.

Mrs. Delmonico was waiting for us in her office.

"What exactly is this all about?" she said as we sat down.

"There have been a lot of misconceptions lately," Dad began. "And a few lies. Taryn is here to clear up as much as she can."

"I didn't order the pizzas," I said. "But I did lie about where I was. I wasn't at the library. I was someplace else, someplace I knew my parents wouldn't want me to be."

"We know where she was," Mom said. "It's a family matter and we intend to punish Taryn for lying. But we'd prefer it if you didn't ask where she was and simply accept the fact that we believe Taryn and we're dealing with it as parents."

"That's reasonable," Mrs. Delmonico said. "And I appreciate the fact that Taryn is admitting she lied to me. I also realize that I caused some of the problems by assuming that Taryn made Mrs. Erdman cry. But it's still just Taryn's word that she didn't order the pizzas—unless there was someone with her, someone other than Lexi, who can corroborate the story."

"I wasn't with Lexi," I admitted. "She saw me

at the library but I didn't spend any time with her. Please don't punish Lexi. I could have said right away that I didn't see her, but I was so grateful for an alibi I let her lie for me. So punish me if you have to, but don't punish her.''

Mrs. Delmonico actually smiled at me.

''I didn't order the pizzas,'' I said. ''But it was my idea. I didn't think someone would overhear me and do it, but now I know that stuff happens. From now on I'll be careful about what I say in public. Yesterday Mrs. Erdman said that no one should steal your thoughts—but people do anyway. From now on I'm going to be a lot more careful about telling people my ideas. For good or bad. Honest.''

Mrs. Delmonico nodded. ''That's a good idea, Taryn. Words can hurt people.''

''And I'm very sorry that my big mouth made someone play a practical joke,'' I said. ''But I think I know who sent the pizzas. I don't want to say for sure because I can't prove it yet. My parents and I worked out a plan, only we need your help. Will you come with us to Mrs. Erdman's room? If I'm right, it should all work out.''

Mrs. Delmonico stared at Mom and Dad.

''It's the best we could come up with,'' Dad said.

better imitation of Taryn than I do. But my Mrs. Erdman is better.''

"It is not," Billy said. " 'Now, class, sit down immediately before I call the riot police!' ''

I was too scared to look at Mrs. Erdman, but I could see that Mrs. Delmonico was paying close attention.

"That's great," Heather said. "You sound real grown-up."

The class hushed for a second. Then I heard Lexi say, "I wonder what's going to happen to Taryn."

"She was suspended yesterday," Nicole said. "Maybe they want to expel her now."

"It was just a joke," Billy said. "Why is everyone making such a fuss?"

"Because she won't admit she did it," Heather said. "If she'd just apologize, she wouldn't be in nearly so much trouble."

"Maybe she didn't do it," Billy said. "Maybe it was somebody else imitating her."

"Then whoever did it should tell the truth," Lexi said. "Before Taryn gets expelled for something she didn't do."

"Taryn and I used to be friends," Billy said. "I never wanted her to get expelled."

"Did you order the pizzas, Billy?" Nicole asked.

The room was quiet for what felt like forever. "I thought it would be funny," Billy said. "I didn't want to get Taryn in trouble. It was just a joke."

"You planned the whole thing?" Heather asked.

"I figured if I used a girl's voice, I wouldn't get caught," Billy said. "And I called from a pay phone in case the pizza place called back to confirm the order. When the phone rang, I used my Mrs. Erdman voice. 'Yes, send those six pizzas right over here.' "

"And Taryn didn't have anything to do with it," Heather said.

"I heard her come up with the idea at lunch," Billy said. "But I did it on my own."

"You should tell the truth, Billy," Nicole said.

"I don't want Taryn to get expelled," Billy said. "But it was just a joke. It'll all work out. I know it will."

"It certainly will," Mrs. Delmonico said as she walked into the classroom. "Billy, you are in deep trouble." Mrs. Delmonico looked at me and my parents. "I'd like you to come to my office," she said to us. "But give me a few minutes to speak with Billy. Let's go, young man."

As soon as Mrs. Delmonico and Billy walked out of the class, everyone started shouting. I ran over to Heather, Nicole, and Lexi and gave them big hugs.

"You were great! Thank you so much!" I shouted.

"I felt terrible saying all those things about you," Heather said.

"But Billy had to trust you so he'd admit everything," I said. "I hated pretending to be mad at you guys, but it's over now."

"Class! Quiet down!" Mrs. Erdman shrieked as she charged back to her desk.

But all of us, including Mrs. Erdman, kept on shouting. And as I stood there, surrounded by my parents and my three best friends, I thought that shouting was the loveliest sound in the world.

Susan Beth Pfeffer's middle-grade novels include *Nobody's Daughter* and its companion, *Justice for Emily*. Her highly praised *The Year Without Michael* is an ALA Best Book for Young Adults, an ALA YALSA Best of the Best, and a *Publishers Weekly* Best Book of the Year. Her novels for young adults include *Twice Taken, Most Precious Blood, About David,* and *Family of Strangers.* Susan Beth Pfeffer lives in Middletown, New York.

IS 61 LIBRARY

IS.61 LIBRARY